"Nothing is as it seems in Seb Doub~~in~~ ~~sky's~~ tale which, like any truly haunted inside than the outside. Beware: it w not let go, and you won't want it to."
– J.S. Breukelaar, author of *The Brid~~e~~*

"Seb Doubinsky's stunning fever dream of a novel, *The Horror*, winks at us from the beginning, playing with genre and form. Everyone knows this story. But do they? With well-earned nods to the horror greats, this prismatic book uses its unreliable narrator who poses dangers of his own—a horror writer who goes to a small town to find still more horror—to foreground questions of truth, history, race, gender, and the unofficial stories that live beneath the official ones. In a thought-provoking twist, the worlds of the novel-within-a-novel, which reflects on the atrocities of World War II, and the book itself intertwine in ways that make us ponder the horror of our own times."
– Caroline Hagood, author of *Misfits*.

"THE HORROR tackles changing presumptions and perspectives, prejudices, and stereotypes of horror novels of the past through the meta and mundane, forcing both readers and the characters to confront the uncomfortable and the too-long persisting realities of racism and sexism."
– Ai Jiang, author of *Linghun*.

"Fear the "normal"! Seb Doubinsky has created settings and characters in situations so terrifyingly normal, that the terror hits with unexpected force, plunging the reader into a churning cauldron of horror by the very ordinariness of everything. Your safety net is gone and you know it could happen to you too, right inside your oh, so safe and "normal" house. Writers' retreats will never be the same again after this!"
– Nuzo Onoh ("Queen of African Horror" & Bram Stoker Lifetime Achievement Award recipient).

Titles by Seb Doubinsky Published By IFWG Publishing International

The Horror (novella)
Turning of the Seasons: A Dark Almanac (with JS Breukelaar)

The Horror

by
Seb Doubinsky

The Horror

All Rights Reserved

ISBN-13: 978-1-922856-66-1

Copyright ©2024 Seb Doubinsky

V.1.0

Printed in Palatino Linotype and Birch Std.

IFWG Publishing International
Gold Coast

www.ifwgpublishing.com

Acknowledgements

As a novel is never just a one-person run but a team sport, I would like to thank my beta-readers, for their support, remarks and advice: JS Breukelaar, Eugen Bacon, Jerry Wilson, John Westberg and Tabish Khair.

I never write in silence and I would like to also thank these artists for the inspirational music which brought out the words, the scenes and the atmosphere of this story: EMA, Angeline Morrison, Shirley Collins, Dave and Toni Arthur, Michael Raven and Joan Mills, Current Pathways and Kim and the Cinders.

I also want to thank my best friend and agent, Matt Bialer, and my wonderful publisher, Gerry Huntman, for believing in and supporting my work.

Kudos to Noel Osualdini and to Steve McCracken for their great editing work.

Finally, last and not the least, special thanks to my wife, Mette Sofie, and my kids, Theo and Selma, for making life stimulating and interesting day after day.

"No, it's not my name. It's a compromise," said Rykte. "Now you have something to call me, but you still don't have a name."

–Brian Evenson, *Immobility*.

ONE
The Place

1

Everybody knows the overused, *cliché* story of the writer coming to a strange town to relax and find some time to finish his or her novel. All have either read the books or seen the films. Many have listened to the audio books. Some have also cringed as they began to read the opening paragraphs or watched the first ten minutes on the screen, thinking, "Oh no, not one of *these* stories again". I know, I was one of them. And here I was, a writer, in a strange town, hoping to finish my novel. *A perfect, boring cliché indeed*, I thought to myself, as I dropped my suitcase on the bed in my rented cabin and looked around the unfamiliar room.

It was rather large, with two windows facing each other, a double bed, a wooden cupboard that looked like an antique. The main room opened on to a small bathroom, with a shower, a toilet and a sink under a frameless round mirror. The main room, like the whole cabin, smelled of beeswax and warmed-up dust, a comforting fragrance which reminded me of my grandparents' house in the countryside. I took my clothes out of the suitcase and distributed them logically in the cupboard, hanging what should be hung (shirts and two jackets) and dividing the rest into the four drawers at the bottom (pants, t-shirts, underwear and four pairs of socks). Taking my laptop out of my other luggage, a sturdy black nylon rucksack, I set it down atop the small table in the central room of the cabin, a long log rectangle which served as a dining room, a sitting room and an open kitchen.

This was my new and temporary castle. I was going to spend the two months of summer here. I felt happy, relieved, expecting good things to happen. I felt in control. Finally.

The past six months had felt as if a permanent storm had raged and wrecked my life. A classic in horror novels too: the main character is in a vulnerable position, his mind ready to be confronted by the unexplainable, an eons-old cosmic curse waiting for him to make all the bad moves. Well, it was almost true. My mind *was* shattered. I had been in a bad single-car accident last winter that had almost destroyed my back. I still felt the pain constantly, although it now had become a familiar presence, like the creaking of wood on an old sailing ship. While I lay in the hospital, Christine, my then-girlfriend dumped me for a younger guy, who was her colleague at the university where she was teaching literature. We had only been together for a year-and-a-half—my divorce had been ten years before, and I was still on good terms with Michelle, my ex-wife—but it did feel like a huge letdown at the time, especially since I was so heavily drugged because of the pain.

As if that wasn't enough, my 16-year-old cat Molly died, which devastated me much more than I would have imagined. Molly had been a faithful companion, a familiar almost, and the sweetest tabby I had ever known. I still dreamed about her often, watching her rush through the kitchen with her sagging tummy to get a bite of raw chicken.

To top it all, my latest novel, *The Dream In The Mirror*, had been a major sales disappointment. What hurt me the most was that I'd thought it was one of my best—and Bill, my agent, had too. The reviews had been mostly positive, but I guess my foray into a more literary style had disappointed my readers. They didn't want subtle ghosts, they wanted bloody demons or possessed serial killers. Something they could relate to, not some weird folklore-based story taking place on a Greek island. I had to accept that my discreet tribute to Lawrence Durrell had failed miserably. My new opus would feed them a heavy plate of traditional horror tropes and characters.

Yes, I felt his was going to be my resurrection.

This was going to be me coming out from the grave where Life thought it had buried me.

This was going to be the summer of all summers, the season of the celebration of life, hope and bestseller writing.

Nothing more, but definitely nothing less.

4

2

It had taken me a while to find exactly the place I wanted, as I was looking for a perfect location at a reasonable price. I needed a place to rest and be inspired, a place where I would feel free and safe, a place that would welcome me with a friendly indifference. All I knew was that I wanted to be by the sea. As I lived in a big city, the idea of a fresh breeze caressing my cheeks while my toes crunched the warm sand seemed ideal. Unfortunately, most of the summer houses for rent during the summer season were way above my means. I had begun to despair, thinking fate was adding yet another heavy stone on my already weakened shoulders when a new offer suddenly popped on my screen. It was the perfect house at the perfect place for the perfect dates. *Too good to be true*, I thought. But it *was* true. And I was there now. I took a deep breath and looked at my new temporary habitat. The sun was shining, the sky was blue, I was surrounded by nature, everything was indeed perfect. The only thing missing was the smell of coffee, and I quickly attended to that.

3

My first impression of the little town had been that it looked like a perfect *Stephen King* setting. As I'd approached, I'd noted small houses painted white, blue, yellow and red were spread among grass-covered sandhills and curving roads. The sky shimmered overhead, like a sublime abstract painting. Parking the car in front of the small general store where I'd been told I could get the key, I realized that for the first time in many months I was actually feeling happy — "not happy-happy, but happy" as the poet Carl Sandburg had beautifully coined it in his poem "Snatch of Sliphorn Jazz". As I got out of my vehicle, a fresh breeze filled my nostrils with the smell of the sea. *Everything is so perfect*, I thought, *it's almost scary.*

4

The woman behind the counter was in her late fifties or early sixties, her beautiful white hair joined in a loose bun held by a pencil. Her eyes were icy blue, but with a sparkle that indicated good humor. She was dressed in an oversized dark red man's shirt and blue jeans, looking relaxed and natural.

I presented myself and she held out a hand.

"Welcome. I'm Clara," she said, with a warm smile which made me feel she meant it. "I have the key for you."

She rummaged in a drawer under the counter and handed me a key with a plastic keyring in the shape of a starfish.

"The house is not far from here. I'll draw you a map. It's very easy to find."

She took out a sheet of paper from the same drawer and took a pen from a cup in front of her. The tip of her tongue stuck out at the corner of her mouth as she drew.

"There you go. It's a five minutes' drive. Lucky you. You've got one of the best locations around here. The ocean is right behind the dunes. You're going to love it here."

I thanked her and proceeded to buy some essential stuff I thought I would need—pasta, tomato sauce, coffee, sugar, milk and a couple of bottles of good wine. The whisky I had brought with me, as I only drank one specific brand and I wasn't sure I would find it here. Glancing at the shelves I saw I had been right. Better safe than sorry, as my mother used to say. I suddenly realized how wise a woman she had been.

5

The drive to the house had indeed been short, but more like ten minutes than five. Through my traveling experience, I knew that locals always tend to underestimate how far places actually are, and this place was no exception.

The house, which was more of a cabin, was even more charming than the pictures on the Web had suggested. It was simple—a yellowish log rectangle with a tiled roof, small square windows with thin white curtains hanging on the sides. A terrace added to the Disney movie feel and let out an impression of happiness and well-being. Surrounded by a large half-circle of low, moss-covered sand dunes, it lay at the end of a short dirt road that shot off the main road and through a pine forest.

I got out of the car with my bag of groceries and I realized I could hear the faint grumble of the ocean. It actually sounded a little bit like the sound of traffic at rush hour, and I smiled at the comparison. *Not very poetic, sir,* I told myself, searching for the key in my pocket as I walked towards the door.

Climbing up the three steps from the terrace, I noticed someone had set a bouquet of blue flowers against the bottom of the door. I put down my grocery bag, picked up the flowers and opened the door. They smelled wonderful. Lavender. One of my favorite smells in the whole world. I had even used it for the title of one of my stories, "The Lavender Boy", about a ghost who left that smell behind him whenever he appeared.

Of course, I couldn't assume that whoever had left the flowers had read the story, but the coincidence was striking. I only hoped that there would be no ghost here. The Lavender Boy was a very, very bad ghost in that story.

6

I poured the boiling water over my instant coffee, added milk and sugar and walked out on the terrace. I took in the view of the dunes, the dirt road, the pine forest, the seagulls circling in the blue sky, the solitary clouds hanging their white heads like tired horses, the sharp but discreet smell of iodine and rotting seaweed, and I let out a long sigh of relief. This was what I had been waiting for for a long time. This peacefulness. I took a sip of coffee and my phone rang, as if to remind me that no matter where I was, the world was still turning—busy, selfish and uncaring.

It was my agent and dear friend, Bill Shapiro. We had been through many challenges together along the years, helping each other the best we could. He had supported me during the last six months, as I had supported him a few years back, when he was fighting against a nasty bout of depression following his own divorce. His first husband had been of the violent and manipulative kind—and a lawyer, which had complicated the legal matters.

"Yes?" I said.

"Hey! Just wanted to know if you had had a safe trip. All good?"

I looked around and smiled.

"Yep. All good. Charming place. Perfect for writing."

"Glad to hear! Can't wait to read it!"

We exchanged a few more banalities before hanging up. I loved the guy. Usually, it's people like him that die in horror stories. The best buddy type. They normally don't last very long. They are put in the story to enhance the dramatic tension. Bill had inspired a few such characters in my past novels. But, of course, I'd never told him.

7

I spent the next few days getting used to my new environment, exploring my surroundings with the thoroughness of a cartographer, mentally mapping all the important spots. I found a gas station, the picturesque harbor with its open-air cafés and restaurants, and, what was more important for me, a locals' bar which I promised I would try to visit as soon as possible; it was also, like the rest of the town, within walking distance from my cabin, although I didn't know if, drunk and in total darkness, I would be able to find my way home easily.

There was also a beautiful house, painted a strange dark red, which dominated the town, perched on a very large dune. It was a sort of a large elongated one-story mansion, which contrasted with the much smaller houses scattered around.

Stranger yet, as I was driving on the outskirts of the village, I found two churches directly facing each other. One was in ruins, only the wooden portal and the front tower remaining, the rest of the building being outlined by flat stones in the middle of a small, charming park. The dates crafted in the now-rusted black iron over the entrance porch of the buildings were different. The ruined one bore "1888" and the other "1893". Both towers were oddly similar, adding a nuance of eeriness to the sight. Loving local lore, I decided I would investigate the matter later, when I got to know the locals better.

I also took long walks on the beach, which was a long stretch of sand and rocks battered by angry, dark blue waves. It looked wild and magnificent, but I guessed the strength of the surf forbade swimming for the inexperienced. I saw a few families scattered here and there, having a windy picnic, and, of course, the local elderly couple walking their dog and throwing a stick as far as their arthritis would allow them.

It was as if a new geography had taken place in my life. I knew it was only temporary, but there was something that felt eternal about it, as if I had subconsciously longed to be here. I wouldn't say it felt like home, but it did evoke long forgotten dreams, perhaps from childhood. It felt as if fate had sent me a subliminal message, and that I had blindly answered its call.

8

The new book was slowly taking shape. I can't say that it was flowing out of me, but it felt easier to write than most of the novels I had written before. I hadn't planned out the whole story, but I had set it during the second world war, and it was about a young German witch named Lili, who is chased by the Gestapo, the Nazi secret police. In my novel, witches had joined the underground to fight against Hitler and were thus persecuted, having to wear a black triangle with a white H (as *hexen*, or *witch* in German) in concentration camps. I had gathered a lot of documentation on German occultism and, of course, on the Reichsfürher-SS Heinrich Himmler's morbid fascination with the subject.

The book was going to be dark and gruesome, but underplayed as far as graphic horror went. Nazism had been horrible enough and trying to illustrate it, or worse, to overdo it graphically, would have been, in my opinion, an insult to the memory of its victims. To transform it into an action-horror story was even worse. I wanted to write a book that would be a politically engaged horror story and not a "Buffy Meets The Nazis" kind of gig.

When I'd pitched the idea to Bill, he was enthusiastic, although he did suggest more Buffy-like scenes. "It would be great if we could sell the rights to Hollywood or Netflix," he said. "Think about that."

In this cabin, Lili was beginning to have a face, a voice, a silhouette. And she was going to kick Nazi ass, but in her own way. Through dreams, invocations and spiritual manipulations.

9

I thought, after the first few days, that I had reached a certain writing cruising speed. I would wake up around seven thirty in the morning, have breakfast and take a walk along the beach. Then I would come home and write (or at least, try to write) for the rest of the day, interrupted only by a quick lunch. In the evening, I would relax with a good dinner, a classic film on TV and a whisky. The only strange thing I noticed was that someone had left another bouquet of lavender in front of my door. I picked it up and put it in a makeshift vase (an empty wine bottle), thinking maybe it was a secret fan that was showing his or her appreciation of my novels.

Not being as famous as Stephen King, I was used both to not being recognized in public places and to be acknowledged in the strangest locations—a park in Paris, the New York subway, a church in Rome. It seemed likely, then, to me, that someone had heard of my arrival and wanted to indicate that I wasn't completely unknown here. After all, the town was small, to say the least, and everybody knows that words travel faster than light. It didn't bother me, and actually warmed my heart a little.

So routine had settled in until one morning, when I woke up to the faint sound of something scratching against my door. I had been dreaming about Molly, my dear late cat, and at first, still lost in my dream, I thought it was her. She used to do that if she felt I didn't get up early enough to give her food, or just because she enjoyed annoying me. Still half asleep, I stood up and mechanically opened the door of the bedroom. A faint breeze whooshed between my legs and I suddenly realized the absurdity of the situation. No cat was supposed to be in the house. I turned around, checked the room, then went to the front door to see if it was open—which it wasn't. I told myself I must have dreamed it, and laughed out loud, but my laughter echoed strangely in the empty cabin.

One thing the mind is excellent at is denial. When impossible things happen, we just dismiss them as impossible and move on.

That's what I chose to do that morning, blaming my dreams and not a reality I couldn't understand.

10

"Are you happy with the house?" Clara asked me later that day, as I was paying for my groceries at the counter.

"Yes, very," I answered honestly.

"It's a good place for writing, I would think."

I looked at her with genuine surprise.

"How do you know I write?" I asked her.

"Well, it's a small town, and you rented the cabin under your real name."

She smiled and produced my latest novel from under her counter. I could see it had been read and dog-eared.

"I loved it," she said, before timidly pushing it towards me. "Would you mind signing it for me?"

I pretended to look for a pen in the pockets of my summer jacket, but she handed me hers and I signed the paperback.

"If I ever find it on E-bay…" I joked, lifting a mock, menacing finger.

"Oh no, not a chance!" she said, grabbing the book and pressing it against her chest. "It will be my treasure now!"

I smiled and was about to leave, when a question suddenly popped into my mind.

"Has the owner of the cabin told everybody in town?"

"Lizzie? Well, no. Not everybody. Just her friends, I'm pretty sure. And that mostly means me."

"Lizzie?" I was perplexed. It wasn't the name of the owner I had signed the contract with, if I remembered correctly. "I thought the owner's name was Thea something. Yes, Thea-Louise Abbott. I remember it because it struck me as an old-fashioned name."

It was Clara's turn to look surprised.

"It must be a joke. Or a mistake. The owner is Lizz… I mean, Elizabeth Nielsen. She lives in the big red house. You've probably seen it. On top of the hill. You should pass by and say hello. I'm sure she would love to meet you. She's the one who got me hooked on your books…"

I mumbled some vague excuses to take my leave and walked out. My illusion of anonymity had been shattered. I couldn't really tell yet if I was vexed or relieved. Probably both at the same time. Vanity versus the comfort zone, the epic inner-soul struggle of the public figure.

11

After having dispatched the groceries to their different compartments in the fridge, I made myself a coffee and turned my laptop on. I looked for the renting contract in my files and checked the name of the cabin's owner.

Elizabeth Nielsen.

It was fortunate I was sitting down, because I felt a powerful spell of dizziness overwhelm me. I was sure that it wasn't the name I had seen on the contract before. Had I dreamed the other name? Could a dream be so vivid that it could make you believe in a self-created illusion?

I had often used dreams in my novels and stories. One of my recurring characters, Ada Faraday, was actually an *oneiromancer*, a "reader of dreams" who used her power to defeat demons and other evil-meaning creatures from the other planes. Still, this didn't explain my confusion. I tried to rationalize, thinking I might have read something about this *Thea-Louise Abbott* which would have mixed things up in my mind, but a quick scan on Google didn't give me any satisfying results.

I knew mental confusion was a sign of mind degeneration, but hell, I was fifty-one years old and had so many tests since my car accident that I felt I knew exactly how fit—or unfit—I was. My memory was intact and I had no problem whatsoever remembering phone numbers, passwords, and how I felt when Christine, my ex, had dumped me while I was still in my hospital bed.

I looked out of the open window, my mug of coffee in my hand. The high dunes and their weird, grassy backs evoked strange animals sleeping under the summer sun. A few birds chirped now and then, and a breeze made the tall grass tufts gently move in the wind like vintage car antennas. A nice feeling of peace finally settled my worries, and I felt that Lili, my new heroine stuck in Berlin in 1938, now could have my full attention.

12

It was late in the afternoon when I finally stopped typing. Lili was still fighting the Nazi regime and its goons, and had just met a young man, Saban, who was a Romani soothsayer, and not a *bohemian* as she had first called him. As he explained to Lili, incorrectly naming someone could also be symbolic murder, and his people, like the Jews, had been misnamed for centuries. Saban thought he knew the secret location of Solomon's key, a magical emerald with incredible powers, and he asked Lili if she would accompany him to Prague, where he thought it was hidden in an abandoned synagogue.

I stood up from my chair and stretched, cracking my knuckles. The moon had risen and shone like a silver scimitar on the sky's deep blue flag. My thoughts were still stuck in a dark apartment in Third Reich Berlin, and I felt like smoking a pipe outside. I had been an irregular smoker since my twenties, and found the occasional pipe a comfort after hours of concentration. Plus I thought it gave me a gentlemanly appearance, especially as I looked scruffy most of the time.

The first thing that caught my eye on the porch wasn't the faint blinking of the first stars as the sky slowly darkened but a new lavender bouquet lying on my terrace. This time there was a small envelope attached, the kind you can buy at florists'. I opened it and took out the little card. It was handwritten, with a very fine and readable script.

"Would love to meet you. Pass by anytime for coffee or tea. I live in the big red house on the hill. Yours, Lizzie Nielsen."

There was a telephone number inscribed on the back of the card, which I slid into my shirt pocket. Lighting my pipe, I thought about my conversation with Clara that morning. I now had the explanation for the mysterious flowers. After the strangeness of late, it was quite a relief.

The evening sky was huge and round, with the moon and the

stars shining faintly. I lit my pipe and let the bitter smoke roll in my mouth like the fog over a mountain.

13

I lay in my hospital bed. I wasn't feeling any physical pain, probably because of the medicine, but my head was still heavy and my vision slightly blurred. It was night and the diodes of the contraptions I was linked to blinked regularly like tiny planets. My mind was full of sadness and catastrophic images. I didn't know what I was mentally hurting most from, the accident or Christine's betrayal, but, once in a while, I would uncontrollably burst into tears. It had happened, for instance, during Bill's visit this morning, when he had held my hand and gently squeezed it. The deep humanity of the gesture, the presence of my best buddy, the weight of the last catastrophic months, had suddenly broken my inner dam and I'd let myself go, wailing and sniffling like a baby boy. Bill had gently wiped my eyes and cheeks and brushed my hair with his lips, like a loving mother. I had always seen myself as a stoic Hemingway and I had suddenly realized I was a pathetic Scott Fitzgerald.

I was alone in the room when the door was slowly pushed open. Not being able to move from my position, I stared at the dark, empty space facing me. The wind? A ghost? Both explanations seemed impossible, but what I saw was even stranger: Molly, my cat, had just entered the room and was looking up at me with that characteristic air of vague interest mixed with utter boredom all felines have.

As I stared at her in utter surprise, she meowed and jumped on the bed.

14

The sudden weight of the animal on my legs woke me with a start and a short scream. I sat upright in the bed, frantically searching for the table lamp switch. I looked around, but saw nothing. I wasn't dreaming anymore, I wasn't in my hospital room but I didn't feel like I had completely reintegrated reality yet. I had felt an animal jump on my feet. I really had.

I got up, and looked under the bed, then checked that my bedroom door was closed. I had fallen from my bed once or twice in my life dreaming I was jumping from a cliff, and I had kicked the wall trying to get rid of a snake biting my ankle. But this had felt so much more real. I checked the bed, lifting the sheet and cover. Nothing.

My heart was beating fast and I decided to get a glass of water. When I turned on the light, I scanned the kitchen, still waiting for an animal of some kind to appear.

It took me a long time to fall asleep again, feeling guilty of being scared of Molly, my favorite cat in the whole world. Then I finally realized the humor of the situation; I couldn't suppress a smile, and finally sank into a much-appreciated, uneventful sleep.

15

I got up late the next morning, woken up by my phone's ring-tone. It was Bill again. We chatted for a little while, and I didn't tell him about my strange experience the previous night. He told me he was thinking about coming up and visiting me the following weekend, and I answered that it was fine and that he would be welcome. Although I enjoyed my solitude very much, it would be nice to see a familiar face.

After breakfast—which was actually a brunch, considering the time—I decided to take a walk on the beach. The sea had always had a soothing effect, and I needed to get that bad dream out of my system. I called it a dream, even though the weight on my legs had felt real. Too real, to be honest.

The sand crunched under the soles of my feet. It was warm, and even with the fresh breeze sweat rolled down my nose. Tourists and locals were scattered around like small nomadic tribes, chatting, laughing, running towards the surf and back. My thoughts drifted to Christine, my ex-girlfriend, still wondering what had happened. I had been in a number of relationships before, some good, some uneven, but with her everything had seemed, for once, perfect. I realized, walking slowly to the crashing sound of the waves, that I was suffering more from my utter blindness than from the loss. It was my pride that had been hurt. It wasn't lethal, but it hurt as much as a paper cut on a knuckle: every time you use your hand, your remember it and wince.

I walked for a long time, then headed for the outskirts of the village across the dunes. I arrived at the twin churches and noticed for the first time the small cemetery that lay behind the ruined one.

It was, actually, a lovely little cemetery, with old tombstones half-erased by the wind. Most of them had turned a rusty brown. I strolled among the stones and my attention was suddenly caught by a spot of blue. A few lavender sprigs were lying on a grave. Intrigued, I walked up to the spot and read the headstone:

"Thea-Louise Abbott. 1873-1892."

I remembered Clara's expression when I had mentioned the name. She would probably have laughed seeing mine now. I walked home in a hurry, my head full of contradictory thoughts. Rather unsettling and unpleasant thoughts, to be honest, and when I arrived at the cabin, I poured myself a tall whisky although it was still early in the day.

TWO
The People

16

I couldn't focus on writing for the rest of the afternoon so I called Bill after dinner to tell him what I had experienced. I was afraid of losing my mind and needed a close friend to talk to. He agreed with me that everything was a bit strange, but told me not to worry.

"You've been under a lot of stress, buddy. On all fronts. Maybe your psyche is reacting in weird ways. You know there's a theory about poltergeists being provoked by the subconscious… Especially with teenagers…"

"I'm not a teenage boy or girl, Bill. And it's not telekinesis. More like really strange coincidences."

"Maybe it's a case of *objective chance*, then? You know, the Surrealists' version of synchronicity? You subconsciously provoke things into happening?"

"Hmmm, yes, maybe."

I hadn't really thought about that.

"Anyway, I think you should find a way to put in into your book," he said. "It would be very spooky."

"Yeah. Whatever."

Typical Bill, I thought, after hanging up. *I know he means well, but he can be so clumsy once in a while.*

I was about to pour myself a comfort whisky, when I changed my mind. I had just realized that it had actually been good to talk to someone. I had been on my own for too long. I needed company, and there was a bar in town waiting for me.

17

The walk to town at night was spookier than I'd expected, because public lighting was sparse along the road. It was the first time I'd ventured outside my cabin after dark, and I had chosen to walk because I knew I was going to be very drunk and didn't want to take the chance of a run-in with the local law over drunken driving. The good thing with the town was that it was really small, and everything was within walking distance, if you considered walking for 45 minutes a possibility. I had lived overseas, in a Scandinavian capital, where cars were much less used than here, and walking was to me as natural as driving was in these parts.

There was no moon and because of the poor lighting, the stars were clearly visible. I remembered H.P. Lovecraft and his descriptions of unfamiliar constellations in strange landscapes. From here, the sky did indeed look much different than in the city: I could barely recognize the Chariot and Orion, now almost invisible against the glimmering background. The night seemed deeper and more dense, as if made of a blend of heavy smoke and luxurious cloth.

The bar with its neon signs looked like a space station in a science fiction film, the familiarity of the human in an alien universe. There were a couple of patrons chatting outside, men and women, some smoking cigarettes, all with glasses of beer in their hands. I passed them and walked through the open door.

The place was larger than I'd thought at first, with a long counter and many tables, small and large, all wooden. It was crowded too, and golden rock-and-roll hits blared from two speakers attached above the bar. The walls were decorated with a mix of rock festival posters, local memorabilia and pictures of various people who I presumed were regular "personalities". One of them was a smiling cop, obviously the town's sheriff, present or past. Another was a smiling Dolly Parton look-alike, which I categorized as "local act", until I saw her behind the counter, attending customers.

"Yes?" she said as I leaned against the polished steel of the counter.

I ordered a beer and a whisky. They sounded like good company.

18

The bar was closing, and I didn't know what the time actually was. I was so drunk I couldn't focus on my wristwatch. Dolly Parton had begun to pile the chairs onto the tables. I clumsily got off my bar-stool.

"Stay safe" she said while I stumbled my way among the scattered furniture.

"You too," I replied, and she gave me a thumbs-up and a smile.

"You can't drive," she said as I banged my shoulder against the exit door frame.

"I'm walking," I said.

"I don't think you can walk, either."

I shrugged, and even this proved somewhat difficult.

"I'll give you a lift. Where are you staying?"

I gave her the address and leaned against the wall, staring wildly around me as she finished cleaning up the room.

When we walked out, she grabbed my arm to lead me to her car, a '90s station wagon. Her fingers felt like warm steel through my thin summer jacket.

"You're not going to throw up, right?" she said as we sat in the car. "I'll roll the window down, just in case. My name's Karen, by the way."

I told her my first name and she nodded as she started the car.

"Nice to meet you," she said. "And welcome to nowhere."

19

I watched Karen's single tail lights disappear in the night and I vaguely waved a polite goodbye. The stars blinked softly over the dark silhouettes of the dunes while a fresh breeze caressed my cheeks. The mixed smells of her perfume, sweat and beer still floated around me, reminding me of my youth and some blurred mornings waking up next to a warm but unknown body.

Shaking my head to get rid of these ambivalent memories, I walked into the cabin, still feeling like I was walking the deck of a sailboat caught in a hard breeze. I turned the TV on and sat on the sofa, watching a documentary on Siberian fauna without actually registering anything of it, except that it snowed a lot and that most of the animals had white fur and behaved badly with the weaker species.

What was left of my consciousness slowly switched to a blurred playback of my drinking session. I saw faces of curious yet friendly people, heard questions, jokes, remembered countless rounds being bought, Dolly Parton slapping one of the guys' forearm, laughing. It had been a good evening in a new place and I now realized I had been needing this without knowing it. I am sure Apollo also got shit-faced with Dionysus once in a while. Logic and rationality can only work better when momentarily plunged into creative chaos, if drinking yourself stupid could be considered creative.

In any case, it worked. I felt better and when I finally turned the TV off and went to bed, I crashed like a Kamikaze plane into a dark and bottomless ocean.

20

I miraculously woke up without a hangover, which was a good thing because my cellphone rang and I could see it was my father. I let it ring without answering. I needed a coffee first. Even though I could call my relationship with my progenitor cordial, it was far from simple.

I was his only child, from a first marriage, with the only woman he ever left—before getting married four more times. His relationship with my mother had been good and, strangely enough, continued so even after their divorce. They'd still talked, up to her death due to a nasty breast cancer a few years back. When he mentioned her, it was always with respect and maybe even (but that might be the son imagining) a shadow of regret. He later became a moody alcoholic—which he still was—but, as a father, I had only cherished memories of a happy early childhood with him. I was five when he moved out.

As a writer, he was more of a crushing figure. He had known an early success with *War And Pieces*, a political satire that had earned him both academic and media recognition. He often told me that it had been both his blessing and his curse. A blessing, because whatever he wrote instantly became a high-brow bestseller, and a curse because he felt that his books were misunderstood, and very often, their meaning deformed. He was both an Olympian writer and a Sybarite, a modern-day Ernie Hemingway for the press appearances and a Norman Mailer for the political braggadocio , although I knew he looked up to Thomas Pynchon and envied his secrecy.

I must say that he always supported my career, even pretending to like the movie and TV adaptations of my books and stories—something I didn't even do myself. But I could often feel, in his tone and remarks, a mean irony concerning my career, which he considered "mainstream", and thus, in his blurry drunken eyes, politically lame and, to put it bluntly, irrelevant.

So, hangover or not, I decided to enjoy my coffee before ringing back.

21

The conversation had been fortunately short, thanks to the relatively early hour regarding my dad's drinking. He was sober and he wanted to know if I could come to the launching of his new novel later that fall. I had already told him yes, but he had apparently forgotten. As tough as he wanted to seem, he had always needed reassurance from his closest circle, something he rarely gave in return.

We never read each others' works, although we pretended to, reaping bits and pieces of the plot on Goodreads and media reviews. It was a gentleman's agreement of sorts, which we respected. I knew my father only read what he considered "top notch literature", and that "Horror" definitely wasn't part of it. I, on the other hand, found intellectual writing pretentious and boring. So that was that.

Hanging up, I thought of him and his new wife, twenty years younger than him—my age, in fact. They had been married for two years now and I wondered how long this one would last. The others had left him because of his drinking, depressive bouts and absolute egocentrism. I was glad that he wasn't a wife-beater, just a genius with a permanent sentimental losing-streak and a complex personality. At least I knew who I had gotten it from.

I sat in front of my laptop, ready for a day's work, trying to get my Oedipus complex in check. To my surprise the computer was in sleep mode, although I thought I had turned it off yesterday evening, before going out. There was an open document too, with two short sentences:

This place is a place of horror.
Thea-Louise Abbott.

I stared at the words without really understanding what I was seeing, except that it was impossible that I had written them. I could admit that I had wrongly remembered shutting my computer—

after all, we do know that memories are often unreliable. But I know I would have remembered writing something down, even in a complete drunken haze, because I had already done it a couple of times in my life. What's more, I never, ever used that font, *Courier New*, to write. And what about my password? Okay, my birth date might not have been the most difficult thing to find, but still... I felt a diffuse fear take hold. Sitting down, I googled the number of the local police station and called the cops. Stalkers could be very dangerous. And not only in *Stephen King* books.

22

The deputy, whose name was John Timmons according to the badge on his uniform, sighed and looked carefully at my front door's lock, then trudged through the cabin to the back door, which he examined too. He was a big man, taller than me, and I'm 6 foot. Black and bald, but with striking green eyes, and a big, bushy mustache.

"You're sure they were both locked?" he asked, suspiciously.

I nodded.

"Absolutely, officer."

"You told me you went out drinking last night. Maybe you forgot to lock."

"I was sober when I left. Plus, I live in a big city so, you know...extra cautious."

The deputy nodded in his turn.

"It's strange, I admit," he said, pursing his lips. "Who would do such a thing? And why? Did you make any enemies last night?"

I shook my head and we walked back into the open kitchen. He looked around, took out his phone and took a picture of my laptop screen.

"Do you think it's a threat?" he asked me.

"I don't know," I answered sincerely, a little taken aback by the question. "It's just an affirmation, with the name of a woman who died long ago. I saw her tombstone at the cemetery."

"Did you? Yeah, it's strange. Is that a pseudonym, you think, or just her name?"

I laughed dryly.

"Well, she died in 1892."

"Yeah, I know that. I meant, could someone be pretending it's her for some reason?"

I shrugged.

"For what reason, officer?"

The policeman looked at me thoughtfully, as if he was wondering if he should tell me something important or not.

"You're a horror writer, right? Famous even, I heard."

"Well, yeah. Not as famous as Stephen King, though," I added, wanting to show him I wasn't pretentious.

"Who is, right? Anyway, I was thinking: maybe somebody admires you and wants you to write about this person."

"Thea-Louise Abbott?"

"Yes."

"What's so special about her?"

The deputy sighed and made his way to the door.

"I don't know, but someone might. I think you should talk to Lizzie—I mean, Miss Nielsen."

"The owner of this place? Why?"

"She loves old stories. She even collects them."

23

Realizing I wasn't going to do my little Lili justice that afternoon in her fight against Nazi scum, I stopped trying to write, cranked up the volume of the background music—which was Wagner's *Siegfried*—for inspiration, got up from my chair and proceeded to do some stretching exercises in order to calm the pains in my back. It was a splendid summer day and the perfectly blue sky had turned my windows into beautiful abstract paintings. The words of Officer Timmons came back to my mind, and I decided it was time to pay this Lizzie Nielsen a visit.

I looked for her card among the stuff spread around the laptop on the table, and read it again. I decided to call her and see if she was still up for a chat around a cup of coffee. It was mid-afternoon, a perfect time to hear some stories about this strange place. Miss Nielsen answered immediately. She said she would be ecstatic if I dropped by. I couldn't resist someone who would feel "ecstatic" meeting me. It was definitely a first.

24

I parked my car in one of the three empty parking spaces at the bottom of the hill. The fourth was occupied by a banged-up and slightly rusty white van which could have been the perfect vehicle for a serial killer. I climbed the soft hill, crushing sand and dried yellow grass under my shoes. The salty breeze filled my senses, refreshing my body under the hard August sun.

The house at the top was a large, one-story wooden antique, painted a nice old-fashioned red, with white doors and window frames. With its little Victorian decorations on the roof, it wouldn't have looked out of place in Norway or Sweden. I stopped before ringing the bell, taking in the beautiful view of the open bay. I also noticed tight tufts of lavender growing on the gently descending slope on the other side, joining the beach at the bottom.

I pressed the doorbell, wondering what Miss Nielsen looked like. I had no idea about her age, but her last name evoked, like the house, Scandinavia, and I imagined a blonde and blue-eyed woman of uncertain age. When the door opened, it took me a second to realize that I was facing an empty space and that I had to lower my eyes to see my host.

Elizabeth "Lizzie" Nielsen was a middle-aged black woman, sitting in a wheelchair. Dressed in a well-cut gray camisole and jeans, her salt-and-pepper hair surrounded her still beautiful face like an aura. She extended a hand, which I shook gently, not wanting to crush her long fingers.

"My, my," she said. "What an honor to welcome you here. Come in, come in!"

She rolled back so I could enter, and shut the door behind me. The house was strangely dark and I realized all the curtains were drawn. Lizzie led me into her living room, a large space crammed with vintage furniture and a jumbled collection of mirrors and etchings on the walls. As I sat down in a comfortable armchair across from her, I noticed the thin bouquet of lavender twigs sprouting from an elongated copper vase.

"Wonderful smell and color, don't you think?" Lizzie Nielsen asked me.

I nodded.

"Yes, wonderful. Thank you for the bouquets you left at the cabin."

She smiled and clapped her hands.

"Tessa! Coffee!"

I felt a presence and turned around.

A teenage girl with long red hair and freckles appeared out of the kitchen, bearing a tray with two steaming mugs, a little bowl of sugar and a quart of milk.

I thanked the girl, who went back in the kitchen. I heard the vague sound of a Youtube channel being turned on, probably on a smartphone.

"She's a sweet girl," Lizzie said. "But not quite there," she mouthed, poking her head with her finger.

"She's your helper?" I asked.

Lizzie shrugged her shoulders.

"She helps me, yes. And very well, I must say. But she's more than that. She lives here. I have, in a way, adopted her. She was living by herself until I... Well, it's a long story. Some other time, maybe. How do you like the cabin?"

"Oh, it's wonderful, thanks. Ideal, I would say."

"It's an honor for me to have you here. I'm your biggest fan."

She giggled in a very charming way and by the way her cheeks darkened, I could see she really meant it.

We kept on talking for almost an hour, drinking coffee and exchanging non-committal opinions about almost everything. Like Clara, she had me sign all of the copies she owned of my books, and as she had every single one of them, my wrist hurt a little when I was finished.

When I left, Lizzie had Tessa come and say goodbye. She joined us holding a beautiful black cat in her arms. As I love cats, I caressed its head gently. It looked at me with complete indifference and yawned.

"I had a cat too," I said, standing in the doorway. "I still dream of her."

"Cats love dreams," Tessa said, as if it was common knowledge.

Lizzie silently repeated the "loony" gesture she had shown me before and softly patted the teenager's back.

Walking downhill back to my car, I thought I had just enjoyed one of the nicest afternoon talks in a long while.

25

My visit to Lizzie Nielsen had for some reason inspired me, and I had no problem concentrating on Lili's fight against the Nazi abomination for the rest of the afternoon. It felt odd to work on this novel, as I had actually begun it a long time ago, when I was still living in Scandinavia. It should have been my third novel, but things had happened and I dropped the project because of too much bad juju attached to it: another girlfriend story gone bad, some minor but annoying health problems and a serious depression right after I had relocated in my home city. I felt that the manuscript was somewhat cursed, and I'd begun working on a new project, which became *Voices In The Forest Of Dreams*, a bestseller, and the first of my books adapted for the screen.

I had picked it up again because after the recent course of events, I felt that Lili's curse had been somehow lifted. Her cause needed to be fought, and I was going to help her triumph against evil. In the scene I was writing, she was using her dream powers to force an SS officer to shoot his heartless mistress and commit suicide. It was very graphic, harsh and sinister, but it made me feel good, to be honest. It was the first time she had used her powers in a lethal way, and they had worked out just fine.

This was the first novel I had ever written with a serious political undertone. Maybe I was going to surprise my readers and eventually shock a few, but I felt like I had to do it, and not because of my father's little ironies. The real world had taken a turn for the worse these past years, and I couldn't consider my role as being only a creator of "pure entertainment" anymore. Given that I didn't tweet, that I wasn't on Facebook or Instagram, I fancied I could still publish words that might make a tiny, yet real difference. At least, I hoped so.

I contemplated the bodies of the officer and his mistress, lying in their bedroom in a puddle of thick, sticky blood slowly soaking the Persian carpet and yes, I felt good. Really, really good.

26

"Welcome back, cowboy!" Karen yelled over the loud music. She smacked a beer down in front of me, and a shot of bourbon.

"On the house," she said.

I thanked her and sat on the high stool. The place was already crowded and lively. It was easy to tell the tourists by their clothes—summery, colorful, loose. Some of them also smelled of coconut oil. They were the loudest, too. Karen was busy behind the counter, working swiftly and precisely. I liked the place, even if I knew I would have preferred it in the winter, when it was empty and gloomy. My father had joked about that when I moved to Scandinavia, almost fifteen years ago: "I am sure you will find Nordic depression to your taste."

The bar was the only festive place open in town, apart from a couple of small restaurants and diners, which made it the perfect tourist attraction during the summer season. But it managed somehow to retain some of its original local personality. Maybe it was the playlist—all classic rock and roll numbers—or the whole *décor*, which was a mash-up assortment of furniture that could have belonged to a 1970s "local cop" series, or maybe it was just Karen herself, but it worked for me. I felt at home and was already thinking of myself as a sort of "temporary but familiar accessory".

A large silhouette, smelling of cheap cologne and deodorant spray, suddenly materialized next to me and I recognized Officer Timmons, dressed in casual clothes.

"Getting the local flavor for your next novel?" he asked, taking a seat on the next bar stool.

"No. Just getting drunk. Writers do that too. Not only cops."

He laughed and offered to buy me a round, which I accepted

on the condition I could buy the second one.

"Now, that could been considered corrupting an officer," he joked, with a deadpan face which morphed almost instantly into a friendly smile.

"Perfect scene for my next novel," I answered.

Karen gave the policeman a long hug over the counter and served us the beers he had ordered.

"So," he asked, "no more strange messages appearing on your computer since this morning?"

I shook my head.

"No, thank God."

"Maybe you have a ghost as a fan? Like Casper, you know?"

I shrugged, smiling at the absurd idea.

"Well, speaking of ghosts, like I told you, I saw a grave with that name, Thea-Louise Abbott, in the cemetery the other day," I said. "Someone is at least trying to scare me, that's clear."

The officer nodded.

"It could be a prank," he said. "You're a famous writer. Some people could feel that their fifteen minutes of fame are on by punking you."

"I'm not *that* famous," I said.

"Well, here, you are. Obviously. Small town, you know. People get bored."

"Any idea who could have done it? Between you and me?" I asked him.

He put down his beer and wiped the foam from his mustache.

"Well, to be honest, that's the thing: I don't. I have absolutely no idea who could have done this. And I'm not protecting anybody's ass here, I swear."

"Tourists, maybe?" I suggested.

"Nah. I don't think so. Look around you—most of them are middle-aged, family-oriented or older. And we have the wildest ones in this place at night."

I turned around and gave the bar a quick glance. Timmons was right. Loud and rowdy didn't necessarily mean young. Another literary *cliché* shot down.

"So…" I said, nursing the last of my beer. "What should I do now, you think?"

Timmons pursed his lips.

"Maybe you should… Wait a minute—want another beer? You're not driving, are you?"

"I said I would buy the second round…"

"I insist."

"Sure. And no, I'm not driving. I'm walking."

"Walking? You're definitely not from here."

Timmons ordered another round, Karen flashing the "OK" sign with her fingers.

"Maybe you should buy some kind of surveillance camera. A small one? Hook it up somewhere in the room?"

I nodded.

"Yeah," I said. "Not a bad idea."

"There's an electronics store in town, near the two churches. I'm sure Mike will have one. He actually has a lot of stuff. Phones, computers, you name it. Wait."

After lifting a finger, he took out a notepad and scribbled down the address.

"Those two churches," I inquired, "what's the story? Strange stuff."

"Have you visited Lizzie yet?"

"Yes. This afternoon, as a matter of fact. But I didn't mention the churches. Just passed by to say hi. We had a lovely talk. General stuff, you know. I had to sign all her copies of my books."

The police officer cracked up.

"Figured she would want that. She told me she was your biggest fan. I must admit I never read your books, although I saw the films. Actually liked them. I didn't know you'd written the novels that inspired the films, to be honest. Lizzie told me that, too."

"I hope she's not a fan like in *Misery*," I joked.

"Well, for one she's disabled, so I can't really seen her carrying you up her stairs. And there are no stairs in her house, incidentally. No, she's a nice woman, even if not everybody thinks so around here."

I looked at him, surprised.

"How do you mean? She's a lovely lady!"

"No to everyone, apparently."

"Why?"

"Local stuff. Rumors. You know how it is."

Timmons gulped down his glass and slammed it on the counter.

"I've got to go now, or the missus will be upset. About Lizzie, ask her yourself. Like I said, she's got stories. Too many of them, even, maybe. She sure can talk until your ears fall off sometimes. And you can call me John, by the way."

"Okay, John. Have a good evening."

He patted me on the shoulder, hugged Karen across the counter one last time and left.

"Another round?" Karen asked as I put down my empty glass.

"No thanks," I said. "I'll make it an early night this time."

"Okay, sweetie," she said. "See you soon!"

I left a good tip and made my way to the exit, thinking about Timmons's suggestions. I liked the guy. Very much. In my novels, however, characters like him always got killed. Always.

27

The twenty minutes' walk home was nice, gradually taking me from the lights of the small town to the half-darkness of the road and the small pine forest. I had to take out my phone and use its LED light for the last stretch, the sinuous gravel path up to the house.

I was inserting the key in the front door lock when I heard a soft sound behind me. Turning around with my phone, I lit the porch, almost jumping up when I saw a dark shadow staring at me, motionless, at the bottom of the stairs. It was a black cat, holding something shiny in its mouth. Its eyes shone flatly because of the phone light, two small silver coins.

It trotted quietly up the stairs and sat again, its eyes never leaving mine. I waited, not knowing what to do. Cats could be friendly one moment, a whirlwind of rage the next if you approached them carelessly. It finally dropped what it had in its mouth, turned around, ran down the steps and disappeared in the night.

I focused the circle of light on the tiny, shiny object that lay on my porch. As I couldn't make it out from where I was, I walked up to it and crouched down to pick it up, feeling the hairs on my neck rise as I realized what it was. A woman's ring. A simple, thin gold ring with a tiny red stone, possibly a ruby. It wasn't the ring in itself that seemed ominous—it was the cat bringing it to me, like an impossible messenger of darkness.

28

"A what?"

"A ring. I'm holding it right now. A woman's ring."

"That a cat brought in, right?"

"Yes, Bill. I know it sounds crazy. That's why I'm calling you at this hour."

There was a pause. I could picture Bill frowning.

"Are you drunk? I mean... Honestly?"

"No, I'm not drunk. Had a few beers at the local joint, yes. With a police officer, mind you. But I'm perfectly clear-headed."

More silence.

"Okay, maybe I should come visit. What do you think?"

"Yeah. I would really appreciate that."

"I'll make arrangements and call you back tomorrow, OK? Is there a hotel in town?"

"Two I think. But they might be full for the season. I have a big couch here, if you can't find a place."

"OK, thanks. Call you tomorrow. 'Night."

"'Night."

THREE
The Friends

29

Bill arrived two days later, and I drove to pick him up at the airport of the main city, which was about an hour and a half away. Nothing special or unsettling had occurred since my encounter with the cat, and I felt a little self-conscious as I drove into the airport's parking lot.

I had kept the ring in a glass in the kitchen, to be sure not to lose it. I had thought about contacting Timmons about it, but the cat story would have been difficult to explain. I still had about six weeks left in the house—and that could be a long time if the locals began to see you as a complete freak. To make things worse, I was stuck in an important chapter of my Lili story, and hadn't managed to come out of the ditch yet.

I needed more whisky and good company. I hurried towards the arrival gate.

30

"Very nice out here," Bill said, looking out of the car's window, as we arrived at the town's outskirts.

"Yes, it's picturesque," I said. "Pine trees, sand dunes, yellow grass and houses painted in different colors. Plus the wind and the sea. Ideal, really."

"How's the fish restaurant? I read good reviews on Trip Advisor."

"I'm not into fish, but we can try it this evening. Just hope they have other stuff, too."

"Always the one sticking out, I can see", Bill said, laughing. "No wonder everybody knows you around here."

"Yeah, right."

Driving into town, I could see Bill taking the whole décor in. Like me, he was a man of big cities. This must have been like planet Mars to him.

"Your hotel is right next to the restaurant, actually," I said. "Well, everything is near everything here."

"Yeah. I can see that. I would go nuts living here, like in a Peter Straub novel, you know: I see ghosts and everybody hates me because I'm lifting the carpet under which the locals buried the corpses…"

I parked the car somewhere near the hotel, and Bill took out his small suitcase. He had told me he could only stay for a day and a half, as he had to attend an important meeting for a film project based on one of his client's book series.

"You know how it is," he had said.

"Yes," I had answered, because I did, obviously.

There were only two hotels in the town's picturesque center, strangely located side by side. One was called The Harbor Hotel and the other The Neptune. Bill had found a room in the latter, which was almost a miracle as this was the height of the season and The Harbor Hotel seemed shut down, its lobby windows covered with cardboard and there was dust on the panes. But

Bill got lucky: apparently somebody had canceled at the last minute, so he had booked a two-bed room for the price of a single.

I let Bill settle in his room and waited in one of the two large leather armchairs of the lounge. The man behind the counter was looking at his computer, probably checking reservations. I took a glance at the busy street outside, filled with the nonchalant, mid-afternoon crowd.

"Excuse me, but you're the writer, right?"

I turned my head towards the counter. The man was looking at me, his eyes expecting an answer.

"Well, yes. I guess I am," I answered, feeling, as usual, both flattered and annoyed.

"I'm Brady," he said. "I'm the owner of the place. It would have been an honor to have you as a customer."

The man looked in his late fifties and wore a sporty polo shirt. He had a deep tan and thinning blond hair. Under his eyes, he had the puffed-up skin alcoholics sometimes display.

"Thank you. I've rented a cabin. Next time, I promise."

"You're staying in Lizzie's cabin, right?"

I was surprised by the sudden change of tone. The question wasn't friendly, but inquisitive. His blue eyes were planted in mine like icy search-lights.

"Is that a problem?" I answered, a little bit too defensively.

Brady shrugged.

"She's not very popular around here. Just so you know."

I noticed Bill coming down the stairs and I stood up to greet him and end the strange conversation.

"I'm hungry," Bill said. "Let's try that restaurant."

"Good idea," I said, hurriedly pushing him out through the door.

31

The restaurant was fine and Bill relished his fish while I had quite a delicious steak. We made small talk and enjoyed each other's company, like old friends do.

His presence reminded me of the city I had left behind, the huge, smelly concrete and glass labyrinth I called home. I realized that I didn't miss it that much—at least, less than I'd expected when I left. In spite of the weird things that had happened here, I enjoyed my solitude and my temporary way of life. This town felt like a time capsule, an interzone between different realities, caught between civilization and nature. And the least I could say that it was inspiring: I had written almost a third of the novel.

Bill said he wanted to have a look.

"I can sense it's going to be your best one yet," he said, ordering dessert and another glass of wine.

"Don't you say that every time?" I joked.

"Yeah, but after everything you've been through, it will be your resurrection. No less. Trust me on this. I *know*."

He made some abracadabra gestures, and winked. We laughed, raised our glasses and deep down inside I really, really hoped he was right.

32

I had been sleeping for a while when I suddenly heard a loud noise coming from the kitchen, like a glass falling and breaking . Sitting upright in my bed, I felt my heart beating faster and remembered the threatening words uttered by the hotel owner. Could someone be trashing my home, because of Lizzie's reputation, whatever it was? I thought about finding a weapon I could defend myself with, but there was nothing I could use in the bedroom. I stood up quietly and tiptoed to my door, which I very carefully opened.

Not seeing anything in the dark and thinking that surprise could give me a strategic advantage, my fingers felt for the electricity switch. In the sudden flash of light, I saw a black cat sitting among the shards of a broken glass. Without looking at me, it picked up the ring in its mouth and ran away through the open front door. I chased after him in the darkness, but could not see it anywhere. Back in the kitchen, I picked up the bits of glass and cut my thumb so badly I suddenly woke up.

33

The pain in my thumb felt real, but there was no cut, nor blood. I was now sitting in my bed for real, trying to clear my thoughts after this new bad dream. The sun shone through the thin curtains, making everything in the room look strangely beautiful. I finally stood up, got dressed and walked into the kitchen. To my great relief, the glass where I had put the ring stood intact next to the sink. I laughed at myself over my panic episode and picked up the electric kettle to boil some water for coffee. As the water ran from the faucet into the kettle, I glanced at the glass again and first thought my eyes were betraying me: the ring was gone.

I shut the faucet and frantically grabbed the glass. Nothing. It was gone. Cursing aloud, I looked around, on the floor, in the sink, under the table, the chairs, to no avail. Maybe that ring had never existed in the first place, I tried to reason to myself, as I prepared an exceptionally strong cup of coffee. Maybe I had been dreaming awake. There was never any cat, nor any ring. It was all in my mind, and I'd believed it was true, for some reason. Yes, maybe it was just an hallucination, a "psychotic episode", as it was called, caused by subconscious stress. *Maybe, maybe, maybe.* These "maybes" rang in my head like an eerie church bell, only momentarily relieved by the dark bitterness of the coffee.

34

"That is really something," Bill said, staring at the two churches. "Do you think they built one, it burned down or whatever and they rebuilt the other right after? And kept the first one's ruins as a reminder, for some obscure reason?"

"Looks like it, yes," I said.

"You should try to find out more about the story. Could be something for you."

"I was planning on it."

Bill shook his head.

"Crazy," he said. "No wonder you told me the place reminded you of a Stephen King novel."

I had picked up Bill at his hotel. We'd had lunch and then he asked me if I could give him a tour of the town. We had slowly moved away from the tourist center and were now at its edges. Behind the churches lay the cemetery and beyond it the dunes and the ocean. We stopped in front of the tomb of Thea-Louise Abbott.

"It's smaller than I imagined," was all Bill said, and I didn't mind.

The ocean was a beautiful sight from the top of the dunes, even if the beach was covered with tourists lying on sandy towels or chatting under colorful parasols.

"This place is truly beautiful" Bill said as we were walking back to my car. "Maybe you should move here and start a writers' colony."

"Nah. I'm like you. Although I'm enjoying being here, I'm still a city rat."

Bill nodded as I unlocked the car.

"I read you," he said. "I read you. I would end up hanging myself here. Too beautiful. Way, way too beautiful."

35

I went on the porch of the cabin while Bill was reading what I had written of Lili's story so far. He had insisted and I had reluctantly given in. I didn't like to show my unfinished manuscript to anyone—to me, a work in progress was just horrible scribbling until it was published. Pipe stuck in the corner of my mouth, arms crossed across my chest, looking at the trees in the distance, I thought with some amusement that I probably looked like the iconic image of the "Writer". At least in the Fifties or the Sixties, when writers still smoked the pipe.

"Wow," Bill said, joining me on the porch. "Wow, wow, wow."

I looked at him, saying nothing, but nervously biting on the pipe.

"It's fucking excellent, man", he said, happily giving me a side hug.

"You said the same for my last novel too," I reminded him. "And it bombed."

"True, but this one will be a major hit, I can tell you. That Lili woman, what a great character! And I love the way you use dreams in this one. So clever. And scary."

"I always use dreams. It's my signature—like small towns in Stephen King."

"Can't wait to see where it goes. You left me hanging here, with her and her Gypsy friend being arrested by the Gestapo..."

"*Romani*, not *Gypsy* or *Bohemian*, as I explain in the novel."

"Yeah, you're right. You're absolutely right. Anyway, it's a great story. Hollywood will love it."

"Sure hope so. Need to pay my hospital bills."

Bill patted my back like a big bear.

"You sure went through some hard times, amigo," he said. "Glad to see you back in the saddle again."

We gave each other a fist bump and walked back into the house.

"I would love to see that ring, by the way," Bill suddenly said as I was taking some beers out of the fridge.

"Well, hmm, I've lost it," I said, handing him one of the cold cans. "Can't find it anymore. I should have taken a picture of it to show you. I feel like I've become the proverbial 'unreliable narrator' now, believe me. And you probably think I'm going crazy, like in all good horror stories."

I laughed, but I could hear my anguish peeking through.

"Nah, you're not crazy. You probably put it somewhere you can't remember. Happens all the time. I just would have loved to see it. What a great story in any case. Is it going to be in your book?"

"Thinking of it," I lied, as we sat on the chairs on the porch.

We made small talk for the rest of the afternoon, under a beautiful blue sky, a few white clouds and with the crazy screams of a lone seagull.

36

"It was great to see you," Bill said, and gave me a long hug. The small airport was almost empty so early in the morning, and I felt like I suddenly was a character in a 1950s flick, when travelling by plane was still a luxury few could afford.

I had picked up Bill at the hotel and had been relieved to find a clerk and not the threatening owner behind the counter. Seeing my old friend and partner had been great. It was the balancing vibe I had needed since my arrival in this town.

I hugged Bill back and saw him off as he walked towards the security checkpoint like a happy bear. On the way back, I stopped by Clara's mini supermarket and bought some provisions for the week, so I could entirely focus on Lili and turn the book into the bestseller that would bring me back to literary life.

37

Getting out of my car, the first half-surprise was the lavender bouquet stuck in the entrance door's handle. The second, not-so-good one, was to realize that I hadn't locked the door. And the third, definitely bad one, was to see my computer turned on. As to the fourth, it was of the worst possible kind: someone had used my computer again to write a crazy message.

> TURN THEIR DREAMS INTO NIGHTMARES, AS
> THEY DID WITH MINE
> THEA-LOUISE ABBOTT

That was when I decided to follow Deputy Timmons's advice and buy a surveillance camera.

38

The computer and electric appliance store was much larger than I had imagined, but I had forgotten that boats need a lot of electronics these days, and there was a short line in front of the counter. Locals for the most part, as far as I could tell. I patiently waited for my turn, trying to understand what the overheard conversations were about, but they definitely confirmed that I wasn't a specialist in boat equipment.

The guy behind the counter was a thin and wiry middle-aged guy, with thick glasses and a silvery buzz cut. Everything in him screamed old Army and sure enough, he had a faded Special Forces tattoo on the inside of his left forearm.

"Yes?"

I told him I needed a wireless surveillance camera for my home. He nodded, turned around and went in the back of the shop. He came out again about two minutes later, with five boxes on top of each other. He explained to me the differences between the various models regarding the number of pixels, memory size, etc. I finally walked out with a mid-priced model, not exactly sure of what I had bought, but glad to escape the tedious technical enumerations.

39

Lili and her friend (and now lover) Saban were detained in the Gestapo headquarters' cells in Prague, and I was confronted with the problem of getting them out of there. A Nazi magician had blocked Lili's dream powers—when she dreamed, she was in an inescapable cell, just as in reality. We were in the early months of 1941 and things were looking grim.

I lifted my head from the laptop screen, massaging my eyes and trying to think of what could happen next. I had only vaguely mapped the book so I could feel free while working on the novel. It had seemed like a good idea at first, but I wasn't so sure anymore. I was beginning to think that maybe I should just write down the whole plot and follow it, like I had done with all my previous novels. Freedom of creation sounded great, until you were stuck in a ditch. Like—right now.

Sighing, I stood up to get a cold beer out of the fridge. Although the surveillance camera I had bought was almost invisible—a small plastic thing set over my bedroom door—it gave me a strangely dissonant vibe of security mixed with a sense of being watched in my own home.

My phone rang and I saw it was my ex-wife, Michelle. I wasn't surprised, as we had kept in touch, but I was curious nonetheless. She told me she had run into Bill yesterday evening at a restaurant, and they had chatted together for a little while.

"So I thought I would just call you up and check on you," she said.

"Check on me? Why? Did Bill get you worried?"

"No, not at all. But he did mention that you were still suffering from the accident. He said it might be PTSD."

Bill! I knew he meant well, but couldn't he keep his big mouth shut once in a while? Michelle was a doctor—PTSD meant something very precise to her, it wasn't just a vague reference.

"Oh no, nothing like that," I laughed, trying to make it sound as natural as possible. "Short bouts of depression, sometimes.

Nightmares. You know the deal."

"Bill also said you were having hallucinations."

I laughed again, admiring my acting talent.

"Oh, he did? Someone pulled a prank on me in the house and I freaked out. I talked to the police. They think somebody is trying to get famous on Instagram by punking me. That's all there is to it."

"Bill said he had come to visit you because you sounded like you were about to freak out."

"Seriously? He said that?"

"Yes, but you know Bill. He isn't always...great with words. His husband, who was there, also said that he was exaggerating and he admitted he was. 'Slightly,' he said. So that's why I called."

I sighed.

"I was pretty shaken, true. But I'm fine now. Seriously."

There was a pause. I could picture Michelle's face as she gathered her thoughts.

"Listen, I'm sure you're right, that it's not PTSD or anything, but maybe...maybe you should see someone when you come back. I have a friend who is specialized in PTSD..."

"I don't suffer from PTSD," I said.

"I just said you probably didn't. But this guy is a great shrink, PTSD or not. He can probably help you. You've been through a lot. We all know that."

I thanked her and ended up the conversation as quickly as possible. I could understand Michelle's concern, but felt it was smothering, as it had while we were married. Although our divorce had been quite a decent and civilized one, it also hadn't been the best time of my life. I decided that what I needed was a drink. A stiff one. And without patronizing company.

40

Walking into the bar, I immediately noticed Officer Timmons chatting with two other men at the counter. They had their backs turned to me. One shifted his posture and I tensed as I recognized the hotel owner who had semi-threatened me. The other man was the computer guy who had sold me the camera this morning. *Small town, small circle of friends,* I thought. I was considering turning around when Timmons noticed me and gestured me to join them.

The officer began to introduce me, but the hotel owner interrupted him.

"Thanks, John. We met before. The famous writer."

"Oh, so that's you!" the computer store guy said, with genuine surprise in his voice. "You came this morning to get that surveillance camera…"

"A what?" the hotel owner said. "What for?"

"Somebody played a prank on our friend," Timmons explained. "I'm glad you took my advice," he added, turning to me.

"Not surprising, given where he's staying," the hotel owner said.

"For sure," the computer guy agreed.

"By the way," Timmons interrupted, "this is Brady, who owns the Neptune Hotel, and this is Mike, who runs the electronics store. Well, you know that already, but you have the names now."

We laughed and shook hands. Timmons bought a round and I noticed that there was another girl behind the bar, a redhead with a bob and tattoos on her shoulders.

"Karen's not working tonight?" I asked, accepting the beer Timmons was handing me.

"No, it's her night off. Tomorrow night too, just in case you came to see her," Mike said with a smirk.

"What's wrong with the cabin I'm staying at?" I asked Brady, deciding to clear the bad air once and for all.

"Not the cabin itself," Brady said, glancing at Mike for support. "The cabin's fine. It's the owner that's a problem."
"Come one, guys. Not that again," Timmons sighed.
"Why?" I asked. "Why is the owner a problem?"
Mike shrugged.
"She's not from here and she's killing this town. Bit by bit, she's shutting it down."
"You don't know that," Timmons said.
"Yes, I do, yes, I do," Mike insisted. "We've got proof. You can ask Jeb."
By the way he slightly slurred the words, I realized he was drunk.
"The supermarket, the garage, the Harbor Hotel, the movie theater, property—she buys it all and lets it rot," Brady said and gulped his beer down. "She wants this town dead."
Timmons shook his head.
"I don't know what Jeb told you, but that is some crazy ass conspiracy theory, if you want my opinion. She bought that cabin, too, and our friend is renting it right now. It's not "rotting", as you guys said."
Mike and Brady exchanged a dark, alcohol-charged look.
"That may be so," Mike admitted, "but Jeb says he has proof she bought the rest. And she's doing nothing with it. Man, the supermarket was bought five years ago! And the movie theater too!"
Timmons let out a long sigh.
"Whatever you want to believe, guys. I'm no part of it."
Brady shrugged.
"Don't let that color fool you, John. That woman is evil."
I felt Timmons tense at the racist slur, but he just took a sip of his beer, looking at me over the rim of his glass. I made a quick nod and raised my eyebrows to indicate I had noticed.
"Next round is on me!" I said, taking out my wallet, hoping to lift the invisible cloud of hate that had suddenly surrounded us.
"Come on, Mike," Brady said. "We can go drink on my porch, between friends, if you get my drift."
I watched the two men walk away, waving at us ironically as they stumbled through the entrance door and dissolved into the darkness of the front parking lot.

41

"Well, that was interesting. And that's an understatement," I said. "What are you drinking, John?"

"A beer, thank you. These guys are actually OK", Timmons said. "Most of the time. But they can get mean when they drink. Then they go on with their conspiracy theories."

"What's the problem with Lizzie Nielsen?"

Timmons shrugged.

"I don't know, actually. Racism, maybe. You heard Brady. Or 'locals versus strangers'. She settled here about six years ago. The rumors were already going full blast when I took up the job. And that was three years ago."

"I paid her a visit last week. She seemed very nice. Her helper, too."

"Nat? Yeah, he's nice."

"No, a teenage girl. Can't remember her name."

Timmons frowned.

"Didn't know she had another helper. Nat must have been sick or away. But, yes, Lizzie is a very nice woman. Quirky, to say the least, but nice."

"Quirky?" I asked. "In what sense?"

"She's not the easiest person to be around, to be honest. I'm lucky, because we hit it right off when I first met her, and yet I can see why she can get on people's nerves. She often acts like she's 'entitled', if you get my drift, and some of the locals resent this. As you could see tonight."

I wasn't sure I was understanding Timmons right.

"Entitled, because she's black, or handicapped, you mean?"

"Black, handicapped *and* rich," the policeman said before taking a long sip of his beer and grabbing the chaser. "Not exactly the best combination in these parts."

I nodded.

"Rich? Is she really buying up the town, as those guys said?"

"Rich enough to live in the most expensive property in these parts and not having to work. I don't know about her buying up the movie theater and the rest. If it's legal, it's none of my business. Anyway, to change the subject, did you experience more trouble since the last time we talked? I just heard you bought a surveillance camera."

"Well, I had a new visit yesterday. Another message on my computer," I said with a shrug, trying to look detached and cool about it.

"Really? Was it threatening?"

I shook my head.

"Not for me, no. But it might be for others, although I don't know who it could be."

"How do you mean?"

I told Timmons what the message said and he rubbed his chin pensively.

"Hmmm, creepy indeed. It would fit well in one of your novels, I guess."

I laughed, a little too eagerly.

"Indeed. It would be perfect."

"I'll keep an eye on your property once in a while."

I thanked Timmons and we bought another round. We raised and bumped our glasses, like the old friends I felt we had just become.

FOUR
The Horror

42

"So, I heard you missed me, stranger?"

I smiled as Karen handed me my beer.

"I was just surprised you weren't behind the bar the other evening."

"Really? Was that all? Now I'm disappointed. That's not what John said."

I laughed.

"Well, in any case, I'm glad to see you."

"The pleasure is mutual. Here you go."

Karen poured whisky in two shot glasses, which we downed in unison. I hadn't been back for a couple of days, and it was true that I was glad to see her again. I appreciated her rough friendliness and I wasn't oblivious to her charms, although I had no desire to have a fling: I didn't feel psychologically solid enough yet to embark into a story that would complicate things even more.

I scanned the place to see if Brady and Mike were around, which would have meant a shortened visit for me: I didn't need any bad vibes at the moment. The writing was going relatively well, and I'd had a good talk with Bill in the morning.

"I didn't know you were a famous writer, by the way," Karen suddenly said, walking back to the end of the counter where I was sitting. "I'm sorry. I don't read much."

I shrugged.

"No offence taken. I'm not that famous, either."

Karen mockingly pushed my shoulder.

"Come on, mister humble! Two films and a TV series! That's famous enough for me!"

"It was a miniseries," I joked, but she had already left to attend another thirsty customer.

The bar was only half-full that evening, maybe because it would be the end of the season soon. I had two weeks left here and I wondered if I was going to miss this place. Karen took my empty glass and put a new beer in front of me. Well, at least I knew I would miss *this* place.

"I heard you also had a little run-in with Mike and Brady."

I shrugged.

"Nothing serious. They don't seem to approve of the place I rented."

"Lizzie Nielsen's cabin, right?"

I nodded.

"They said she was killing this town by buying places up and not doing anything with them."

Karen shrugged.

"I wouldn't know anything about that. If they're thinking about the supermarket and the cinema, they were already closed when she bought them. Same with the hotel. *If* she bought them. Their saying, not mine."

"Well, in any case, Lizzie's cabin is very comfortable," I said. "And inspiring."

"Glad to hear. Hope it will give you some ideas for your next novel."

I raised my glass to her and chugged what was left of my beer.

"Another one?" she asked. "It's on me. I want to show you this place can be hospitable, too. Inspiring in a good way, not just a horror novel way."

43

I was drunk and sitting comfortably in Karen's car. Her shoulder bumped into mine once in a while when the car hit a small pothole. I didn't mind, and I enjoyed the short whiff of perfume, deodorant and sweat that came with the soft shock of her body.

It was nice of her to drive me back again, and I told her.

"No problem," she said. "You're a nice customer. Not that many around here. What's more, John likes you, and I like John."

Muddled thoughts formed in my mind.

"Are you and John…?"

Karen laughed.

"No. Not that I would mind, to be honest. But he's married. And faithful, the dork!"

I nodded vaguely.

"You're married?" she resumed.

I shook my head.

"Was. We're still friends, though."

"Girlfriend, then?"

"No. Not anymore."

I smiled, although I felt a pinch in my heart.

"You're a handsome man. And famous. Women must hound you," Karen said, with a sly wink.

I didn't really know where this conversation was going, but at this very moment I only wanted to get home and crash on my bed—alone. I liked Karen, but I really didn't want things to get more complex than they already were for me.

Her right hand suddenly landed on my knee and stayed there. I was thinking how to get myself out of this tricky situation without hurting her feelings when a shape suddenly appeared in the headlights in the middle of road.

I screamed something and Karen brutally veered to the left. There was a tremendous shock and an incredible pain flared in my right shoulder and chest as my body was stopped in its flight by the safety belt. My head hurt too and it took me a couple of minutes to come back to my senses. My eyes slowly refocused and I realized someone was standing in front of the remaining headlight. A small woman or a teenage girl in a strange dress was pointing at something next to me. Her face seemed to reflect the light and her features seemed blurred. *What the hell?* I thought, wincing with pain.

Slowly and carefully turning my head to the left to see what the girl was pointing at, I saw Karen's head resting on the steering wheel. Her eyes were open in the darkness like light gray half-moons, and bubbles of spit and blood appeared now and then at the corner of her mouth. She was softly moaning in pain.

A sudden and inexplicable rush of joy and hatred filled my head and body, an exhilarating feeling of sheer power and rage that I had never experienced in my life before. I grabbed her hair and banged her head on the steering wheel until I heard the bones of her nose and skull crack and give in. When I finally stopped, I was breathing heavily but my thoughts were crystal clear and focused. I was now sitting in complete darkness and silence, in a wrecked car wrapped around a tree. My left hand was covered with blood and a revolting mix of sticky bits and hair. I had just killed someone and I was feeling great. I was feeling like having a whisky on the rocks and a cigarette.

44

I woke up with a start in my own bed. The first thing I noticed was that my head and right shoulder hurt like hell. Images of the gruesome nightmare kept flashing under my eyelids. I had never experienced such an evil dream before. I looked down at my body and felt my eyes trying to register what they were seeing: an enormous bruise covered my chest on the right-hand side. I felt it with my fingers and a flash of pain exploded in my brain. I tried to remember how I got into bed, but everything was blank. My last memories were of being chatted up by Karen at the bar. And that was it—apart from the nightmare.

I slowly got up, trying to come to my senses. I walked into the bathroom and examined myself in the mirror. The bruise was large, but I couldn't tell where it had come from. The most reasonable explanation was that I had walked home in a drunken haze, stumbled upon a rock and fallen against a street light or a tree. Or something along those lines. The nightmare must have come from my own accident, six months ago—a subconscious flashback that also probably involved my feelings about my ex-girlfriend, embodied in the dream by an unfortunate Karen.

Slightly reassured by my own instant psychoanalysis and feeling more focused after having splashed some cold water on my face, I decided that a strong coffee would do me good.

The first thing I noticed as I walked into the open kitchen was the single sprig of lavender on the table next to the laptop. Perplexed, I went to pick it up, but my hand stopped in mid-air: the laptop was turned on and somebody had written a message again.

ONE.
THEA-LOUISE ABBOTT.

I was awake, but the nightmare continued. I took a deep breath, trying to make sense of what was going on, trying hard to remain logical and rational in spite of all this craziness. I told myself once again that I'd just had a nightmare caused by my traumatized subconscious. That this was still a prank which, by sinister chance, seemed somehow connected with that horrible dream. This word, "One", could mean so many things, right?

And then the phone rang.

45

It was Timmons.

Karen had died in a car crash last night. He thought I would like to know. Freak accident, on a totally straight stretch of the road, on her way home. They were still waiting for the lab results about alcohol in her blood, but he doubted that it could be the cause. He knew her well and she would have called a cab if she had felt too drunk to drive. Yes, it was terrible, she had been a good friend. He would miss her.

"Me too," I said, sincerely, and he hung up.

Sadness grabbed my heart and squeezed it slowly between its ice-cold fingers. Maybe the dream had been a premonition, mixing with other emotions that I had managed until now to suppress.

I hurriedly made myself a coffee, hoping the bitter liquid would give me some strength, and I sat down in front of my laptop, looking for the file containing the surveillance camera recordings. I knew that the answer to one of the mysteries lay there, and I wanted to know who was trying to make me go insane.

I clicked on the play, then fast-forward symbols, and waited. I saw my own silhouette stumble in and slowed down the video. I held my breath as I walked past the table with the laptop on, half expecting to see myself sit down and type the message as in any psychological horror classic. But I did walk directly into my bedroom and the time was 23:33. My heart beating a little faster now, I clicked on the fast-forward symbol again until another silhouette walked into the room at 00:06.

A small and narrow-shouldered girl or young woman, dressed in an old-fashioned manner, hair pulled up in a tight bun. It was the same silhouette who had appeared in the headlights of Karen's car. Her face was unfortunately blurred, although the rest of her was clear enough for me to make out some details—the long skirt, the tight blouse with the larger shoulder pads, the black ribbon attaching the bun.

Cosplay, perhaps? I watched her bend over the laptop, type with one finger and leave. My first reflex was to grab my phone, but I put it down again before I dialed Timmons's number. What would he make of the message? Could I tell him about my dream? What if he wanted me examined by a doctor and he or she saw the bruises on my chest and shoulder? Wouldn't it be easy to connect them with the marks of a safety belt?

I deleted Thea-Louise Abbott's message, changed my password again, and decided to check who in the hell she was and why she was plaguing me.

46

After having googled "Thea-Louise Abbott" and the name of the town a couple of times in various ways with no result whatsoever, I decided to call the local paper and ask if I could check their archives. When they inquired about the reason for my interest, I gave them my name and said I was working on a horror novel which would be based on real facts which took place here at the turn of the nineteenth century. The woman on the line said that it sounded very interesting, but as the paper had been established in 1953, she couldn't help me.

I took a shower to clear my mind, but I felt as lost afterwards as before. While I shaved, I toyed for a few minutes with the idea of following my ex-wife's advice and call that doctor she had mentioned for a consultation. But I finally sat down on the porch in the morning light, watched a couple of tiny black birds fly by, and patiently waited for panic to decide to leave my body like an exhausted demon.

47

Realizing after a while that I wouldn't be able to concentrate on my novel, I decided to go have a brunch in a café by the harbor. The place was crowded and lively, which kept my mind nicely distracted from the dark clouds hovering over it. I ate some fried fish and fries with a chili mayo, which were excellent by tourist town standards, and ordered a coffee. I called the waiter and as I took out my wallet to pay, he told me that some "gentleman" had already paid for my bill. Surprised, I turned around in the direction he was indicating and saw Brady eating alone at a table in the far end of the café. He saw me glancing at him and signaled me to join him, which I did, hoping he wouldn't notice my reluctance.

"Thank you for getting my bill," I said, standing by his table, wanting to spend as little time as possible with him.

"I just wanted to make amends about the other night. We were drunk and, well...we got carried away. Very sorry about that. No hard feelings, I hope."

I shook my head.

"No, no hard feelings at all".

"I know you're not responsible for what's going on in this town. But me and Mike and a few others, we've had enough of that bitch. Pardon my French. So...we got very pissed off and forgot our manners. We can be like that sometimes. Karen might have told you. She knows us well. We all go back to high-school days. The 'Wild Bunch', they called us."

I nodded, and hesitated before opening my mouth again.

"Did you hear what happened to Karen, by the way?"

He stopped eating his club sandwich.

"No, what happened?"

"She... Well, she died in a car crash last night."

Brady suddenly turned very pale, except for a hard blush on his cheeks.

"Oh no... This is terrible! Terrible!... Who told you?"

"Timmons. He called me earlier this morning. He thought I would want to know."

Brady nodded in silence and I left him there, a crushed soul sitting alone at a café table, staring at a half-eaten sandwich.

48

The indifferent sea looked picturesque under the infinitely blue sky. A few puffed-up clouds rolled from west to east, pushed by a crisp breeze. Fragments of conversations, laughter and screams rose from the multitude of tanned bodies on the beach, some of them hidden under colorful parasols. Watching this ideal summer vacation scene, I suddenly realized I was still in shock from the news of Karen's death and that terrible nightmare. My shoulder and chest still hurt, and I had taken a strong paracetamol to quell the pain. My back felt sore too, feeding my mind with flashbacks of my own accident, six months ago.

I decided to walk away from this unbearable happiness and blessed ignorance, and I took to the dunes. The weight of my painful body sinking into the grassy sand was exactly what I needed. It coincided perfectly with my reality—the struggle, the slow way forward, the short, gasping breath. Little by little the happy noises of the beach faded, replaced by the exhilarating nothingness of the breeze, the mumble-grumble of the waves and the occasional scream of a distant seagull.

Since childhood, I'd always enjoyed walking alone. My thoughts were my invisible friends, answering my questions, comforting me if I felt bad, celebrating with me if I had a good grade (my mother didn't care about this sort of thing) and were good at small talk. I can imagine that people who believe in God or in gods and goddesses share the same experience, with the added supernatural aura. But angels, demons or spirits were not for me. I never believed in anything, and I still didn't. Death was a big black hole and nothing could come back out of it. Never, ever. That was it. The end. Kaput. But today, my thoughts weren't exactly my friends. Rather, they banged against the window pane of my conscience like terrified birds.

As I walked among the dunes bordering the town, I remembered Michelle's advice to go see a shrink. Maybe I wasn't as strong as I imagined, and she might have seen another part of me that I was trying to ignore: anguished, panicked, prone to hallucinations. The worst part of it all was that if I admitted wholeheartedly that I had been seriously shattered by the last six months, I still couldn't admit that I was, to some degree, losing my mind like in a classic H.P. Lovecraft story. I had not seen any forgotten gods, the stars shone in their right place in the night sky, and there was no strange curse plaguing the town. Everything was trivial and normal, from the local animosities to Karen's sad and tragic death. And what I had experienced could very well be self-induced delusions triggered by some nasty prankster. As my father always said, with a glass of whisky in his hand: "The real explanation is always the dullest." And that was precisely what I wanted to believe at this very moment.

49

I finally arrived at the two churches, and decided to visit the standing one. Although I had walked among the ruins of the other and enjoyed the pretty garden they had built around them, I had actually never entered the relatively newer one. I also wanted to go to Thea-Louise Abbott's small tombstone one more time afterwards, to see if the prankster in costume had left me any clue. After watching the disguised silhouette on my computer screen, I had half-convinced myself I had been pulled into a local macabre riddle.

I had just tried the shiny round copper handle when a voice resounded behind me, giving me a start.

"It's closed."

I turned around and my surprised must have been apparent because the young man standing in front of me lifted his hands up in the air as a peace offering.

"I'm sorry, I didn't want to give you a shock. The church is closed. I'm Thomas Burns, the parson."

I presented myself and we shook hands.

"Oh, you're the writer!" the man exclaimed. "I saw the movies they made out of your books. Liked them very much. Both of them. Honored to have you here. Would you like me to give you a tour of the church? It's quite small, to be honest."

Before I could answer, he had taken a set of keys out of his pocket and swiftly opened the door.

"We have begun to lock it recently. Some vandals came in one afternoon and sprayed graffiti and did some minor damage. Satanist stuff. Kids, probably. You can get tragically bored here in the winter. And as the French poet Baudelaire famously said, "Boredom is the worst of fiends"..."

The parson smiled. He was quite tall and thin, with freckles and red hair, dressed casually. Handsome, in a very healthy and reassuring sort of way. Perfect for a man of the faith, I thought, although I would have never thought of him as a priest if I had seen him walking down the street, just a "normal kind of guy from a small town somewhere."

"First time I've heard a priest quote a decadent French poet," I said as we walked into the building, which was a shock of white, enhanced by the summer sunlight.

"Who had the reputation of being a Satanist, to top it all," Burns said, with a side smile. "Oh well, I went to college before finding my vocation. I was a French major and wrote my master's thesis on Baudelaire."

That explained that. He gave me a short tour as he had promised, showing me around this rather banal building. I nodded politely once in a while, pretending to be interested. There was no sign of the vandalism he had mentioned, and I asked him about it.

"We painted over it," he explained as we were walking out. "Like I said, there wasn't much, actually. A couple of pentagrams, some poorly spelled mumbo jumbo in Latin, and they pissed on a cross they had detached from the wall. That one."

He pointed at a large crucifix between two windows.

"It was in the local paper, if you're interested. Maybe an idea for a novel?"

I smiled and shrugged.

"Yes, why not?" I answered politely. "But I am actually more intrigued by this church over there. Or what's left of it."

"Oh, that's a great story, actually," Burns exclaimed as if he was really happy to have finally found someone to tell it to. "Very dramatic. There was a fire during a funeral and people died. Five, I think, or maybe more. The stories differ. But one of them was the priest, Father McKenzie, and the funeral was his wife's. How about that? He went back to save some people trapped in the flames, and the roof came down. He's buried in the cemetery with his wife, behind the church. But that's not all, or rather, that's not the story itself."

He paused, looking at me with a smug smile. I told him to carry on, which he did enthusiastically.

"They tried to rebuild the church, but there were many accidents. Deaths even, it is said. Couldn't rebuild it, couldn't destroy it. The new priest, O'Toole, said 'OK, let's build another church then, and forget about the old one'. Which they did. There are many legends around that church. Local lore. Hauntings, curses, you know the deal."

He winked at me.

"Are there ghosts attached to this church?"

Burns nodded, looking at the ruins.

"Yeah. There is a 'White Lady' walking alone among the ruins by moonlight. They say it's a young girl who perished in the flames and who is looking for her parents. And the parson and his wife, walking hand in hand. That sort of things. Ghost stories are always heart-breaking."

"That ghost girl, does she have a name? Thea-Louise Abbott, for example? She's a young woman buried in the cemetery. Same death date as the burned church."

The parson shrugged and shook his head.

"Nope. Well, I don't think so, I mean. I just heard the story and the girl's ghost has no name. Just a poor girl aimlessly walking in the ruins of her church. Never seen her myself. But it makes great conversations at night, around the barbecue."

"Have many people seen her?"

"Some say they have, indeed. Last time was just a few months ago. But it's a very local legend. I don't think anybody knows about it beyond this town but, like I said, it could be some good material for a story of yours."

"Yep," I agreed politely, thinking, *oh boy, if only you knew.* But I just thanked him, exchanged a few more words about the weather, shook his hand and was on my way.

50

Thea-Louise Abbott's tomb was the same as the last time I had visited it. No message, no hint, just a gray tombstone with her name and dates, decorated with a few drying seagull droppings.

What do you want with me? I asked in a very low voice.

There was no one around, but I knew the wind could carry words a long way, and I didn't want to add ridicule to my anguish.

I have done you no wrong. I don't even know who you are. Or were. If you can hear this, leave me alone. I need my peace, I need my sanity. I don't mean you any harm and I want you to leave me alone. Thank you.

I picked up a twig of lavender and laid it on the grave. Although I didn't believe in anything, I most sincerely hoped she had understood my entreaty.

As I walked away, I remembered the parson's story about his colleague from another century who was killed in the fire in his church trying to save members of his flock, and I decided to check if this legend was legitimate.

It only took me a few minutes to find the tomb, as it had the largest and most imposing tombstone of the whole cemetery, made of shiny black marble. Engraved in small golden letters were his name, father Thomas McKenzie, and his wife's, Betty McKenzie born Suter. Their birth dates were different, eight years apart, but their deaths had indeed occurred the same year as Thea-Louise Abbott's own demise — 1892.

I found a few more tombstones with the same year of death — eight in all — but of course they might not all have happened on the same day; only the years were inscribed.

On my way home, my mind weighed down by thoughts, hypotheses and impossible conclusions, I spotted Lizzie Nielsen's remarkable cottage at the top of the hill and remembered John Timmons's words about her collecting all sorts of local stories. The story of Parson Burns had definitely whetted my curiosity, and I wanted to know more. Or rather, to be perfectly honest, I *needed* to know more.

51

Before I could ring the bell, the door opened and Tessa's face appeared in the gap.

"Come in," she said. "I saw you coming up the hill," she added, reading the surprise on my face.

There was a pleasant lavender smell as I walked into the house, mixed with other subtle flower fragrances. Although it was still early afternoon, the place was bathed in a golden half-obscurity because all the curtains were drawn.

Lizzie was sitting in an armchair, back to the door, but her lovely face turned towards me and she smiled.

"What a delightful surprise!" she said. "Please, take a seat! Tessa, can you make us some coffee? You would like some coffee, wouldn't you?"

I sat down in the armchair facing her as Tessa disappeared into the kitchen.

"I had a feeling you would come by," Lizzie said, putting away the book she was reading.

"Really?"

"Yes. I don't know—sometimes I'm like that. I feel things. You know, 'coincidences', people call them."

She giggled, and I smiled too.

"How is the writing going, if I may ask? Is my cabin still to your liking?"

A good, heartening smell of coffee drifted from the kitchen, and I decided to tell my landlord the truth.

"Well, I don't know if Officer Timmons has told you, but someone has broken into the cabin while I was out. Twice, actually."

Lizzie covered her mouth in surprise.

"Oh my God, no, he didn't tell me! Was anything stolen? Or broken?"

"No, don't worry. I would have called you, of course. They only used my computer to write me some weird messages. Timmons thinks it might be a prank of some kind."

"I'll call and have the locks changed immediately. I'm so

sorry! Were the messages threatening?"

Tessa walked into the room, carrying two cups of coffee on a lovely silver tray, along with some milk and sugar.

"I am going out to pick up some flowers," she said.

"Yes, dear, you do that. You always bring back the most exquisite bouquets."

I saw Tessa open and shut the door quietly behind her, letting a brief ray of pure sunshine into the house.

"Tessa loves flowers," Lizzie explained. "And so do I. I earn my living with them, did you know?"

I shook my head.

"No, I didn't."

"I have an online company. We sell flower and plant extracts. Amazing how much healing power they have. Also spiritual and psychological. I studied chemistry and botany at the university. Perfect combination. It triggered my passion, which I turned into my business."

The front door opened again and a slightly disheveled young man in his early twenties walked in, carrying two heavy grocery bags.

"Sorry I'm a bit late, Lizzie," he said as he walked towards the kitchen. "I met a friend on the way who I haven't seen in a while. I'll check your fridge for your dinner tonight. I was thinking something with chicken and rice."

"You're a darling, Nat. Chicken and rice is always good," Lizzie crooned. "My helper," she told me in a half-voice. "Comes in every two days".

I heard the young man in the kitchen opening and closing the door of the fridge, then rummaging in the cupboards.

"I'll go to Clara's and get what I need," he said, appearing in the doorway.

Lizzie grabbed the purse at the foot of her armchair and took her pocketbook out.

"Here's the card. Don't forget the receipt."

Nat made an army salute and walked out, bouncing on the soles of his feet.

"Lovely young man", Lizzie said. "A bit of an airhead, but a fabulous cook. He's the son of the local parson. I don't really need him that much, but he's good company."

"Father Burns? I just met him on the way to your place."

"Oh, really? Lovely, lovely man."

"He gave me a tour of his church and told me a little bit about the other church, the burned-down one."

A thin black cat suddenly jumped on Lizzie's lap, and began to purr as she gently stroked its back. I hadn't seen it coming and it felt like it had appeared from nowhere. *Cats,* I thought, *always ready to surprise you, one way or another.* I suddenly missed my old cat, Molly, and her furry warmth on my knees.

"Ah yes," the woman said. "The burned-down church. This place is indeed full of stories."

She leaned a bit closer to me, but before she could say anything, Tessa was back with a mixed bouquet of wildflowers and lavender twigs.

"Oh, how beautiful!" Lizzie exclaimed.

"I'll get a vase and put them on the table," Tessa said, walking past us.

"I'll tell you later about the church," Lizzie whispered to me. "Tessa is very impressionable. Come back tomorrow or when you can."

I nodded, and Tessa came back with a small vase. She bent over to arrange the bouquet and I noticed that she had a small ring around her finger, which shone flatly in the half-light.

"That's a nice ring," I said, trying to sound as natural as possible, as I had recognized it as the one the cat—*this cat?*—had brought me at the cabin.

Tessa stood up, her face beaming.

"Oh yes, I love it. I found it in the cemetery and Lizzie told me I could keep it."

"Oh yes, dear. I don't think that the owner would mind very much."

For a second, it seemed that my soul was shattering. Feeling violently nauseated and dizzy, I hurriedly thanked Lizzie for the conversation and promised I would drop by again soon.

The sun welcomed me with its cyclopean eye, staring at me mercilessly as I galloped down the hill like a panicked mouse in a hurry to find the safety of its hole.

52

Was I really going insane?
 Yes, said the blue sky towering over me.
 Yes, said the clouds, as they rushed by.
 Yes, said the houses, watching me with all their windows.
 Yes, said the cars with their radios turned on.
 Yes, said the seagulls, laughing hysterically.
 Yes, yes, yes.
 And yet, my mind said. *And yet…*

53

Finally back home, I sat on the porch of the cabin, lit my pipe and opened a cold beer. I needed to collect my thoughts and become rational again. There were many explanations for Tessa's ring, the most logical being that it just looked the same as the other but wasn't it. Just like the black cat that had brought it to me that day. All black cats look alike. That was it. I decided not to focus on the impossible, but on the incredible, just like Sherlock Holmes. A detective of my own life, with a seemingly impossible case to solve. And no Watson in sight. Just me and my computer, instead of a violin, and a cold beer instead of cocaine.

I was taking a long sip of the mild liquid drug when the phone rang. Checking the screen, I saw it was Bill. My own Watson, but so far away. He just wanted to chat, and we did. It was good to hear his voice, which held me connected with the former, undeniable reality of the city. My city. We talked about the weather, the town, my novel, his husband's new fascination with ancient Egypt after they had visited a new exhibit at the city museum.

"Watch out for curses," I joked. "Egyptians were famous for their black magic."

"Protective magic too," Bill replied. "Maybe you should look into it."

I sighed.

"Yep. Maybe I should."

"More problems?"

I could hear Bill's uneasiness in his voice, not knowing whether I was going to speak about *real* problems or imaginary ones.

"Yes and no. I found the ring again. You know the one I told you a cat brought in? A teenager was wearing it."

"Really? How did she get it?"

"She told me she found it at the cemetery. Pretty fucking strange, if you want my opinion. And she has a black cat."

There was a confused silence on the other end of the phone.

"You're right. It is strange. Probably a string of improbable coincidences. Or she stole it from the cabin."

I took a sip of my beer.

"Yes, my thoughts exactly."

"At least you know the ring exists. And that means you're not crazy."

"True. I hadn't thought about it that way, but you're right. Thanks."

When I hung up, I didn't care if Bill had been polite or if he had meant what he said. I felt better, relieved, lighter. I wasn't crazy. I had proof. The ring was real. And that was all that mattered for me at the moment. Reality: 1, Paranoia: 0. I could live with that for the moment. Hell, I could live wonderfully well with that for the moment.

54

The next couple of days went by without incident, except for another black-cat-with-a-ring-in-its-mouth nightmare. But this bad dream had fortunately no consequence in real life, nothing out of the ordinary happened, allowing me to get back to my novel.

Lili had managed to escape from her prison, but her lover Saban had died under torture and had revealed the location of Salomon's key, the magic jewel opening the gates to the apocalyptic power of the heavens. Things were bad, and they were about to get worse.

I stopped writing, feeling sorry for Lili. She was helpless, alone and vulnerable. Her only hope was the Witch Coven of Prague, but I knew she would be betrayed by one of her companions and handed back to the Gestapo. It seemed the horror would know no end. We were now at the end of 1941, and Hitler seemed stronger than ever, marching his troops from Hell towards Moscow.

I made myself a quick bachelor's dinner—frozen pizza and a bottle of red wine—which I didn't enjoy much. I realized I missed drinks, good company, and mindless chit-chat.

Karen's face floated before my eyes as I thought about going to the bar again. I felt guilty although I was certain that I hadn't really killed her. It had been a coincidence, linked with a cryptic prank. I would go to the bar, and drink a few to her memory. This new idea made me feel a lot better. Yes, I would honor her memory by my presence in her bar. The best reason an alcoholic could find.

55

Seeing Timmons's large back at the bar immediately made me feel better. He was in civilian clothes, talking with the bartender that I had met the week before Karen's death, the red haired girl with the tattoos. I noticed the picture of Karen on the wall now had a black ribbon set across the upper right corner.

"Hey," Timmons said as took up the empty space next to me at the bar. "Good to see you."

"Same here", I said, meaning it.

I ordered a beer.

"Chilling after a hard day's work?" I asked him.

"Yeah. Just after a normal day's work. Unless you've got something for me?"

We laughed, him more sincerely than me.

"No, don't worry. No more episodes," I lied. "Just the usual boring writing routine."

"I'll have to read one of your novels, one day. My wife said she read one a couple of years ago and enjoyed it very much. She has good taste: she's a teacher."

"High school?"

"Yes. The one in Greenfield. It's the...uh, suburb of this place."

"Really? I thought the town was all there was. Then again, I'm like all the tourists, I guess. Only see the picturesque parts."

Timmons nodded.

"This place is more complicated than it seems," he said, with a pensive frown. "Took me a while to understand it. Not sure I do yet."

"How do you mean?"

Timmons shrugged.

"Look around. See many black people around here?"

I turned around. I counted two, at different tables, each in a group of young people.

"Two," I said.

"And they're probably not from here. All the black people

remain in Greenfield. Their choice, people here would say. But, like I told you, it's goes deeper than that. Let's just say I'm tolerated here because I'm the deputy."

I shook my head.

"I had no idea. Everything is so charming here, at first sight."

"Yeah, it is. But it can be ugly, too. Like everywhere, I guess. You come from the big city. You know the deal. Hell, you write horror stories. You write about evil. You're a goddamn specialist!"

We chuckled sadly and emptied our glasses. I ordered two more. *The good thing about evil in fiction*, I thought, *is that it remains fiction.*

Timmons abruptly changed the subject, and we evoked Karen's memory, with him telling me anecdotes and funny stories. It was a quiet evening, filled with gloom and friendship.

56

I came home before midnight, feeling drunk and melancholy, but not depressed. I liked Timmons very much and was glad he had considered me a friend, enough to share so many stories with me. When I finally crashed after watching an episode of a popular series that I found atrociously boring, I fell head first into a comfortable nothingness which I hoped would last until morning.

Alas, I suddenly woke up, feeling strangely oppressed, as if an invisible weight was crushing my chest. I felt a presence next to my bed and turned my head in panic. The young woman in the strange vintage costume was there, standing in the shadow, holding a small cat in her arms. It was impossible to see her face and I could only make out general details that gradually appeared as my eyes adapted to the darkness. I was paralyzed by fear, feeling my heart was about to explode and the proverbial cold sweat beginning to run between my shoulders.

"Who are you?" I managed to growl. "What do you want?"

My words came out deformed, as if my tongue was melting and my lips made of burning wax.

The woman put the cat down on the bed and I felt it land on my legs, but I was incapable of pushing it away. She lifted a finger to her lips and I saw a ring briefly glint in the moonlight.

"Shhh," she said softly. "Shhh."

She delicately took my hand in hers and held it for a short while. I couldn't feel anything—her hand was neither warm nor cold, it was simply around my fingers, pressing them slightly, as if it was made of solid air.

"I came to tell you that you haven't lost your mind, my good man. You are only a tool of justice. I know it is a task that is difficult to bear, but you'll soon be free. I promise. Now sleep in peace."

She stooped and blew on my eyelids, which immediately felt they were made of lead. She smelled faintly of lavender.

57

The morning found me strangely refreshed, although the dream or hallucination lingered clearly in my mind. Even if what the apparition (I liked the word better than "ghost", or even worse, "spirit") had said didn't make any sense at all, I felt relieved. If my own mind was playing tricks on me, at least they weren't *completely* dirty—it signaled me that I was still, relatively, sane. Or at least, rational. "You haven't lost your mind". I let that sentence run round and round my brain, savoring it like a good drug. It sounded true. It sounded believable. It sounded as real as a good dream could.

After a solid breakfast and a quick scan of international news on the internet, I decided to let Lili rest for a few hours and explore more of the region. Timmons' s mention of Greenfield had made me curious and I wanted to know more about the social realities of this seemingly idyllic little town.

Greenfield was, as Timmons had said, indeed "well hidden", as it was separated by a large park in the north of the city. The only link between the two urban entities was a long stretch of poorly kept concrete, which looked more like a country road than an avenue. I drove around the area, which was the predictable mix of middle-class houses and run-down habitations. As it was summer, people hung out on the sidewalks or on the lawns, all of them blacks. Shops were open, bars were letting the usual drunks in and out, the school and high school were clean and imposing. There was no sense of dread or despair coming out of the place, but the "normalcy" of an everyday, effectively segregated reality was, in itself, more terrifying. I wondered where Timmons and his family lived. I would have liked to stop by and say hello, but I remembered that the policeman hadn't invited me to come over. Better let things take their natural course, I thought. I could always write my impressions down in a novel, maybe to give myself a better conscience by symbolically denouncing a situation I was unwillingly but clearly part of, because of my own skin color and the history of oppression attached to it.

I thought about my father and the clear political stands in his fiction. He had always been a glowing radical, with a social agenda he promoted via satire and the grotesque. He had become commercial and a darling of the media by accident, because of the surprising bestselling success of his first novel, *War And Pieces*, way back when. Since then, sitting on his borrowed throne, he had enjoyed the incredibly ambiguous position of the revered, envied and slightly feared court jester.

It was strange for me to see our paths come closer after all these years. Maybe it was because of the accident, maybe because I had suddenly become aware of the fragility of my own humanity; in any case I knew now that *Hexen* would not be a stand-alone, but the beginning of a series of far more political novels. I wrote horror, and what was politics, after all?

58

L ili had been recaptured and sent back to Berlin. Because of her
extraordinary powers, she had been taken to the Gestapo headquarters, under the direct supervision of Himmler. Fortunately
for her, the Nazis only knew of her limited ability of predicting
the future, and not of the complete extent of her dream-control
possibilities. This was for her like a knife a prisoner manages
to hide from his guards. She had to be careful to hide her
powers well, as the Gestapo and the SS employed mages and
turned witches to control their psychic human guinea pigs. The
irony of it all was that Hitler himself was a skeptic, a complete
atheist who only believed in himself and in his misunderstood
Nietzschean philosophy. Karl Ernst Krafft, a Swiss astrologer
who successfully predicted an attempt on Hitler's life, was
arrested and sent to a concentration camp in 1941, at the same
time Lili was transferred to Berlin. Himmler had to put a lid on
his own beliefs to avoid enraging the Führer.

1942 was a crucial year for Germany, a time when Hitler
still thought he could win it all. The Japanese were victorious
all over Asia, England was suffering under the V-1 flying
bombs and the German troops were advancing fast in Russia.
However, some crucial strategic choices had to be made as the
Eastern front was so extended that Germany couldn't run the
risk of losing their quickly gained advantage.

In order to promote himself and his esoteric studies,
Himmler thus decides to present Lili to the Fürher.

After a series of tests in which she predicts the future quite
accurately, Hitler chooses to trust her and asks her what his
next move should be on the Eastern front. Lili tells him to attack
Stalingrad, knowing perfectly well that this will be a disastrous
move for the Nazis. Lili briefly enjoys a few months of freedom
before the disaster becomes blatant. She is arrested again and
sent to a concentration camp. Her train is mistakenly bombed
by the British Air Force on the way to Buchenwald, and she

miraculously escapes with a few of her companions. The book ends with her arriving with the Russian troops in Berlin in 1945, and indicating to them where Hitler's bunker lies.

It took me the rest of the week to finish the manuscript, and I felt exhausted. I had only eaten frozen pizza and taken a few walks by the sea in order to have some motion. The final evening, I turned off my computer, stood up, stretched, put another frozen pizza in the oven and poured myself a whisky. Then, later, satiated, a little drunk but still high on writing adrenaline, I decided to go out and celebrate. I was finally free from Lili, free from her nightmare and the Nazi horror. I was back on track, the bastards had lost and this book would put me back in the top selling list. It would be the best kind of book too: a bestseller with a message. And who knew? My father might even read this one.

59

As I walked into the bar, I noticed the place was almost empty. Only a couple of tables were occupied, most of them by young people—students, I guessed, because of their age and the variety of styles and colors. The red-haired bartender smiled as I approached the counter.

"It's pretty quiet tonight," I said, stating the obvious.

"It's a Sunday and it's still early", she answered, also stating the obvious.

I sat on a stool and ordered a beer and a double shot of bourbon.

"I'm celebrating tonight," I said, wanting to have a conversation with someone. I felt like I had walked out of prison and had to become social again.

"Oh yeah? What?"

"Finished the first draft of my novel."

I knew I probably sounded like a five year old kid proudly showing a doodle to his teacher, but I didn't care.

The waitress nodded.

"Cool. I heard you were some hotshot writer. Movies and all."

Before I could pretend to be humble, she turned around, grabbed a bottle and poured herself a shot.

"Congrats," she said. "I guess that's big. So, you find this place inspiring?"

"Yeah, it is . In a weird kind of way, sometimes, but yes."

"I hear you. Half picturesque, half hick."

"You're from here?"

"Yeah. But moving to the big city soon. Just got admitted into med school."

"Wow, that's great," I said. "My turn to congratulate you."

We chatted some more, but I was the only one who kept drinking. I learned her name was Janet, but that everybody called her Jan.

The place had become much more crowded, all of a sudden, and Jan drifted away from me to attend the thirsty patrons pressing themselves against the bar.

A heavy hand landed on my shoulder.

"Look who's here! Our favorite writer!"

Mike and Brady were standing next to me, grinning. They waved at Jan and ordered two beers.

"Cheers!" Brady said.

"Cheers!" I answered politely.

I could smell liquor on their breath. They obviously had begun early.

"How is the cabin treating you?" Brady asked.

"Fine. I just finished my manuscript today."

"Cool," Mike said. "Congratulations. I hope you'll mention us in the book."

"It takes place during World War II, in Europe," I answered.

"Feels strange drinking 'ere without Karen," Brady interrupted, visibly not keen about talking literature. "You liked her, didn't you?"

I nodded.

"Yes. She was a very nice woman."

"Good looking too," Mike said. "Jan is okay, but not the same hotness, if you see what I mean."

Jan was within hearing range, but I hoped the general bar rumble had covered Mike's remark.

Brady scanned the place.

"Lots of nice ladies tonight, though," he said, chugging his beer. "Eye candy."

Mike nodded.

"A sight for sore eyes. Holidays are always good for pussy fishing."

They chuckled and I felt it was time for me to go home. I got off my stool and was about to take my leave when a young black woman stepped before me, a few paper napkins and a pen in hand. She was attractive and I could see the leer on Mike and Brady's faces. She politely asked me if I was the author of the Ada Faraday series. I nodded and smiled at her.

"I was wondering if I could get your autograph. Me and my

friends are big fan of yours."

She pointed at a table covered with empty beer glasses where two other girls were sitting. They politely finger-waved at us, looking slightly embarrassed.

I felt Mike squeeze himself between me and the girl. He put one elbow on my shoulder, the other one on Brady's, and just stared at her with a crooked smile.

"You're a lucky man," he said, without turning his head. "Pussy magnet."

I ignored him and took the girl's napkins and pen, and turned around to find a free space on the bar to sign them. I suddenly felt pushed to the side and heard the girl protest. Brady had grabbed her by the waist and tried to kiss her cheek.

"We're his friends," he said. "You can be nice with us, too."

I pulled the girl by the arm, put myself between her and the two assholes and handed her the signed napkins.

"Sorry about that," I said.

She nodded, thanked me and skipped back to her table.

"Sorry about what?" I heard Mike growl behind me. "Sorry about what?"

I sighed and shook my head.

"I'm leaving, guys. Thanks for the company."

Mike suddenly grabbed the collar of my shirt.

"Sorry about what?"

I thought Brady would pull his friend back, but he only came closer to me. I tried to pry Mike's fingers off my shirt. He squeezed harder and shook me once.

"Hey!" I said.

"You don't like us very much, it seems," Brady said, his face close to mine. "Is it just us or white people in general?"

"Come on," I said. "This is ridiculous."

"Friends with Timmons and that bitch Lizzie Nielsen, and now that sweet black chick—but giving us the cold shoulder? A coincidence? I don't think so."

Jan suddenly saw what was going on and tapped on Brady's shoulder.

"You guys crazy?" she yelled over the counter. "Stop this right now or I call the cops."

Mike finally let go of my shirt and turned around to speak to Jan. I took advantage of the distraction and quickly walked out. I saw, in passing, that the girls had left, too.

60

Lying on my bed with my laptop, I tried to watch a Netflix series, but my mind was racing, still shocked by the evening's events. It wasn't so much the violence that shocked me—I'd had a pretty wild youth with a good collection of fistfights, and I thought I could defend myself pretty well as long as weapons weren't in the picture—but the reason for it: the deep-rooted hatred and malicious envy that it seeped from. I had to admit that it completely paralyzed me with fear, and made me think that I should re-write some passages in my novel with that in mind.

Feeling restless, I stood up to pour myself a large whisky in the hope that it would help me fall asleep. I saw on the cooker's clock that it was a little past 23:00—too early for me to crash, too late to really do anything—so I decided to sit on the porch outside and procrastinate. There was a beautiful full moon and a lukewarm breeze brought in the mixed smells of iodine and seaweed.

My thoughts were slowly drifting back and forth from Lili to this peaceful moment when my ear caught the sound of a vehicle driving up the road towards the cabin. Soon lights illuminated the tops of the trees. Maybe Timmons was coming up to pay me a visit, although it couldn't be good news if it was this late. I stood up, glass in hand, feeling my heart beat faster as the sound of the engine grew closer.

A white pick-up truck finally appeared and screeched to a halt a few feet away from the cabin. Loud FM music poured through the open windows. The doors opened and my blood froze when I recognized Mike and Brady stumbling out.

"Hey! Mister writer!" Mike yelled. "We've come to celebrate with you!"

Brady lifted his right arm. He held a bottle of Jack Daniel's. Under his left was a six-pack of strong beers.

I said nothing and nervously watched them come closer.

"You finished your book! That's something!" Mike added as he stepped onto the porch, grabbing my arm and pushing me back into the cabin.

"Yeah," Brady said, behind me. "And you're going to leave soon. That's something to celebrate, too."

61

"**B**eautiful place you have here," Brady said, standing in the middle of the dining-room, still holding the beers under his arm. "That bitch Lizzie's got taste in decoration, I'll give you that."

"Sit down," Mike said, pushing me onto one of the two armchairs. "Give me your glass. I told you we're going to celebrate."

"Well, I was just about to crash, actually".

I could hear the stress and fear in my own voice, and I'm sure the guys could smell my sweat.

"Come on, now. Show some hospitality, the same as this town showed you."

He snatched the glass from my hand and filled it with bourbon to the rim.

"Hey, Mike! That's the camera you sold our friend?"

Mike looked at the round plastic ball over the door.

"Yep. That's the one."

Brady put down the beers on the kitchen island, then jumped and grabbed it.

"You think it bounces?"

"Gee, I dunno," Mike said, playing stupid.

Brady threw the tiny camera on the floor with all his strength. Some bits flew in the air. Brady chuckled.

"You sold him some shit, Mike. It doesn't bounce at all."

He crushed it under his shoe.

"Real Chinese crap", he said, opening a can. He took another, which he handed to Mike.

"Drink up," Mike said, opening his own can.

I reluctantly brought the glass to my lips and took a sip. Mike quickly held my hand against my mouth in a precise and brutal gesture. I felt the glass hit my front teeth.

"No, no, no!" he said. "Not like that! Drink UP!"

Brady grasped my head between his hands from behind. I was

forced to swallow and I gagged on the hard liquor. I struggled to stand up as Mike was refilling my glass, but Brady slammed me back into place.

"You know what the problem is with these hotshot writer people, Mike?" Brady said, as some more liquid was forced into my mouth and down my throat. "They just don't know how to behave in small towns like this. We could've been friends. You could've stayed in my hotel, you would've made my place famous and I would've shown you a good time with Mike. We know the best eating joints around, we really do. Local food for gourmets. But no..."

"Please," I pleaded, feeling my mind become number by the minute. "I will come back and stay at your hotel. Make this place famous. I swear."

Another glass. I half-puked on myself, making Mike and Brady laugh.

"You decide instead to hole up in this shitty cabin owned by this black bitch who is herself holed up in her own shitty mansion on top of that shitty hill... She's buying the whole town right under our own noses, and we can't do shit... Timmons won't look into it because he's black too and they have this solidarity... But we checked it out... The fund that bought the supermarket, the movie theater, the hotel, it's the same one... And it's owned by Flower Life, which is owned by... Yes, you guessed it right! That bitch Lizzie Nielsen!"

"I don't have anything to do with this," I gurgled as I watched with horror Mike fill another glass. "It's your problem, not mine!"

"Well, now it *is* a little bit your problem, it seems, right?" Mike said, signaling Brady to hold me tight as he forced more bourbon into my mouth.

"This town is dying, a big shot like you could've helped us get some publicity, you know, talk to the local paper, take some pictures with us, but no... You just ignore us and try to humiliate us in our own drinking hole... Man, you're directly insulting Karen's memory here..."

"I don't think she would like you very much right now," I managed to splutter.

Mike punched me in the stomach, a quick and precise jab that made me instantly throw up. Brady's iron grip tightened even more.

"Listen, asshole… Karen was our friend, since high school… A real party animal and a part of the team… You have no idea what we've done together… We miss her every single day, and you…you…"

He slapped me so hard I felt my lower lip burst, and sparks exploded before my eyes.

"What do we do now?" Brady asked.

Mike took a step back, holding the hand that had slapped me.

"Now we make our town famous," he said.

62

Mike beat me up some more, until I passed out. When I woke up, Mike and Brady were shoving me onto the back seat of the pick-up truck. Everything hurt and I couldn't move.

"Should we tie him up?" I heard Brady ask as they climbed into the vehicle.

"Nah. He's so drunk he can't do shit, and we shouldn't leave any marks. We'll dump him far enough for the currents to take him away, so it'll be a while before they find him, all bloated and shit."

"Right," Brady said. *"Famous writer goes for a midnight swim and drowns in beautiful harbor.* I can see the news. Perfect."

"That should attract some attention," Mike said, starting the engine. "This place could become as famous as the Keys with Papa Hemingway."

"You bet," Brady said. "Let's go to the boat."

These were the last words I heard before I lost consciousness again.

63

"WHAT THE FUCK?" Mike screamed and I felt like I was suddenly flying.

Everything tumbled and rolled in a deafening mixture of crushing metal noise and the screams of Mike and Brady.

Then everything stopped and silence fell.

My whole body hurt and the smell of gasoline filled my nostrils, making me gag. I was in complete darkness.

A door suddenly opened and a ray of moonlight struck my eyes.

"Come," a voice said.

I knew this voice.

"I can't move," I explained.

"Now you can."

I miraculously felt well again, as if all the broken bones of my body had been mended. I didn't feel drunk anymore, either. I sat up and climbed out of the wreck.

Brady's bloodied body was half out of the windshield, while Mike was huddled on top of his friend. They were both groaning softly and repeating useless "fucks". I recognized the road. It was the same place as Karen's accident.

I suddenly realized I was standing in a puddle of gasoline and took a few steps back.

The young woman was there too, the cat in her arms. I wasn't surprised. Her face was clearly visible now. Tessa. She pointed at something. A Zippo lighter, which shone in the moonlight. Mike's or Brady's, probably. I nodded to her, knowing what she wanted me to do.

I picked up the Zippo and rolled the flint wheel with my thumb a couple of times until a small blue-and-yellow flame materialized. I threw the lighter into the gasoline puddle. A sudden flare illuminated the night, and my face felt warm.

The moon was incredibly beautiful, unsoiled by Mike and Brady's inhuman screams.

64

The morning sun found me waking up in my armchair, in terrible pain. I could feel my head throbbing, both inside and out. *I am a murderer*, I thought. And yet my conscience rejected this thought with all its might, refusing to accept, or even consider it as a possibility. *A bad dream*, I told myself, slowly getting up from the armchair, wincing with every move. *Another nightmare. Just another nightmare.* Standing up and looking around trying to clear my mind, I spotted the empty bottle of bourbon on the kitchen island and the crushed beer cans littering the floor. I carefully smelled my fingers. They reeked of lighter fuel and the meaning of "nightmare" suddenly shifted for the worst.

I walked into the bathroom to take a look at my face. I looked like an amateur boxer who had lost his first fight. Although I was afraid of what Timmons might tell me, I decided to call him and make a complaint. I'd almost convinced myself that I must have blacked out after the beating, and that the rest of it was a nightmare.

The officer picked up immediately.

"Yes?"

"John, Mike and Brady stopped by my cabin last night and beat me up. I want to press charges."

There was a short silence and I realized he was outside, with people talking in the background.

"Well, they're dead. Both of them. Car crash. I'm at the scene. Looks like they were burned alive. We'll talk later."

I hung up and looked at my bruised face.

Murderer, I thought, and I felt an icy river of panic flow into my veins.

If I had really been on the crime scene, I must have left DNA traces, footprints, even. And my fingerprints on the Zippo. Who would believe me if I said that a teenage girl I barely knew made me do it? That I was hypnotized or telepathically manipulated into burning Mike and Brady alive?

I remembered Tessa's expressionless face... I had to talk to her.

I walked into the dining room again and saw that my computer was on the table. I knew it had been in my bedroom when Brady and Mike arrived. A knot in my stomach, I turned it around. It was switched on. And, of course, there was a message.

THANK YOU.
GOODBYE.
THEA-LOUISE ABBOTT

There was also a yellow post-it stuck on the laptop screen: "I know you will need to talk. Come and visit. Lizzie".

I looked around me, not knowing anymore where I was.

Tears welled in my eyes and I didn't stop them from rolling down onto my cheeks.

FIVE
The Stories

65

Nat opened the door and started back, seeing my face. He immediately apologized.

"I'm sorry," he said. "But your face..."

I didn't answer and followed him in. Lizzie was in her usual armchair.

"Oh my! What happened to you?" she said as I sat in front of her. "Would you like a glass of cold water?"

"No, thank you. It's a little difficult for me to drink."

I pointed at my swollen lower lip.

"Of course. I am sorry."

Nat passed by, putting on a light summer jacket.

"I'm on my way, Miss Nielsen," he said. "I'll be back around five."

Lizzie waited for the sound of the door shutting before resuming our conversation.

"Tessa is not around?" I asked, wanting to sound detached. "I would have liked to speak to her."

Lizzie gently took both my hands in hers.

"Tessa is not going to come back, precious."

"She ran away?"

Lizzie sighed, still holding my hands.

"No, she went home. At last. Thanks to you."

I thought I might be suffering from a mild concussion, as nothing seemed to make any sense anymore.

Lizzie let go of my hands and picked up a thick photo album from the ground, which she put on the table between us.

"Now, dear, I am going to ask you to have an open mind. A very, very open mind."

66

"My archives on this town," she explained. "As you can see, I am quite the collector".

She went to the first page and her finger pointed at the photograph.

"Now look carefully," she said.

There were three people in the picture: a man, a woman and a girl servant. The man and the woman were seated, both dressed in black, with a stern look on their faces. The girl stood behind the man, in black-and-white servants' attire. The caption read: "Father McKenzie, his wife Betty and their maid, Thea-Louise."

"Thea-Louise Abbott," I murmured. "So that's who she was. And…she looks a lot like Tessa. Are they related? Same family?"

Lizzie looked at me right in the eyes.

"No, my dear. This is Tessa. Or rather, Tessa is Thea-Louise Abbott."

"What?"

I felt my heart bang against my ribs like a terrified animal.

"This is ridiculous!" I said, deciding to leave before everything became too weird for my shattered conscience.

Lizzie grabbed my hand in hers again, holding it firmly.

"I told you you had to keep an open mind. I have some stories to tell you. All I can say is that you are not crazy, and I am not crazy, although you might think otherwise when I am finished. But if you don't listen to me, and you leave right now, you might very well become crazy, because your mind will never understand what really happened."

I sat down again.

"Okay, but just know I don't believe in ghosts, or anything supernatural."

"It's not a question of belief, dear," Lizzie said, calmly. "It's a question of seeing and, most important, of accepting."

She kept my fingers trapped in hers, stroking the back of my hand as if I were a child. It wasn't condescending, though. It felt motherly and caring.

"I might write ghost stories and horror novels," I resumed, "but they're pure fiction. I don't even believe in God. I'm a radical atheist."

"God has nothing to do with my stories, as far as I know," she said, with a half-smile. "And I'll get back to your novels later. Right now, I would like to tell you the story of Thea-Louise, her death and the two churches."

67

"**Y**ou see, my family comes from this town. Way back. My great-great-grandfather was the judge here, in the late 1880s. And no, he wasn't black—I will get to my own story later. His name was Ben Sprague, and he told my great-grandmother the story, and she passed it own to her daughter, who told it to my father, who told it to me. It is a family story, and it will die with me, as I have no child.

Thea-Louisa Abbot was a slightly mentally deficient child, who worked for the McKenzies. John McKenzie was the town's parson, and Betty, his wife, did charity work. The official story goes like this: Betty found out that Thea-Louise had stolen her ring and hidden it under the clothes in her drawer. Thea-Louise, either because she was terrified of having been discovered or mad with rage, had violently pushed poor Betty, who fell down the stairs and broke her neck. Thea-Louise tried to run away, but was captured by a mob of righteous citizens led by the parson, who had been in the house downstairs when his wife was killed. The mob became enraged and strung poor Thea-Louise up a tree outside the town. End of the official story. You can read it here. It's not from the local paper, but it is how the story was told."

She turned the page and showed me a copy of a newspaper article.

"You mean that Thea-Louise was lynched by the mob?"

Lizzie Nielsen nodded slowly.

"Yes, and it is as horrible as it is. Fortunately, I have the unofficial story, told by my great-grandfather to my grand-ma. And it is even grimmer. Thea-Louise didn't run away. She went directly to the judge's house because she knew she had done something horribly wrong. Her face was bloodied, and her nose was broken. She told my great-grandfather that Betty had beaten her with a metal hair brush. She had discovered the ring in her drawer and was absolutely furious."

"So she had stolen the ring?"

Lizzie lowered her eyes before looking up at me again.

"Thea-Louise told my great-grandpa that the ring was hers. That Father McKenzie had given it to her to thank her for 'being nice' with him."

"Am I understanding this right?"

Lizzie nodded.

"And so did my great-grandpa. The girl was slow in her head, and the parson had taken advantage of her. My great-grandpa decided this was worth a fair trial, and decided to put her in the jail for the time being. But they met the crowd, led by the parson, in the streets. You know the rest. That's where the official and unofficial stories meet. With the hanging of a poor teenage girl on the outskirts of the town."

"Wow," I said, knowing that it was a stupid word, but my brain couldn't come up with a better one at the moment.

"But are you ready for more?" Lizzie asked. "We are still under the sunlight, but now comes the time of the moon."

68

"Betty McKenzie's funeral was scheduled on the Sunday following her murder. All the town was there, including my great-great-grandpa, his wife and my great-grandmother, who was five at the time. The weather was stormy, with black clouds rolling across the sky and a very heavy wind. When the ceremony began, lightning struck the tower at the entrance and the roof began to burn. There was a panic, and everybody ran out as the fire spread. My great-grandfather and his family were lucky to be near the entrance, so they made it out. Many didn't, as the roof crashed, killing Father McKenzie and a number of citizens.

"After the disaster, rumors began to spread, linking the fire to Thea-Louise's lynching. Some said they had seen her ghost the day of the funeral, or laughing above the collapsed roof. My great-grandpa didn't believe in any of this rot, but some events made him change his mind.

"When the town council decided to rebuild the church, they discovered it was an impossible task. There were unexplained accidents, tools got lost or broken, and there was even one death—a carpenter who fell from his ladder. Some said he was the one who had put the rope around Thea-Louise's neck. People were as religious as they were superstitious in these parts, my dear, so it was decided to leave the old ruin alone and build a new church. Are you following me?"

I nodded, not knowing where these old tales were leading us, and my soul felt muddled with a disagreeable mix of curiosity and dread.

"This town was cursed," Lizzie said, sitting back in her armchair. "And it still is. I am the living proof of it."

I frowned and winced because of my bruises. Without a word, Lizzie slowly lifted the bottom of her blouse. The large bright pink scars were like horrible paint strokes on her brown skin. I said nothing, tantalized by the sight.

"I was adopted, as you might have guessed now. My parents

were liberals, who believed in equality and chances for all. I don't think they had realized what sort of town they really lived in. Have you heard of Greenfield?"

I nodded.

"Yes. John Timmons told me about the area. I drove through it. I see what you mean."

Lizzie took a deep breath.

"Good. Blacks are tolerated when they stay in Greenfield. Oh, don't get me wrong: this town has never been segregated, not officially, at least. But until thirty years ago, you didn't see black people drinking in the bars by the harbor or eating in the fancy fish restaurants. Not to mention that mixed couples were unheard of, or pressured out of town. My father was the high school principal. He thought he could change things. He really thought he could. My mother did, too. But they couldn't. My childhood was lonely, to say the least, and I didn't make many friends in school. It got worse when I got to high school. I got sneered at, laughed at, or, even worse, totally ignored. Then, one day, a miracle happened."

She stopped, joining her hands as if she was praying. But her eyes were hard.

"I was invited by a girl called Karen to a party at her house. It was incredible. I was so glad. And so were my parents, God bless their souls. Karen was a high school star, the knock-out blonde all the boys chased after. That night, I took my most beautiful dress and drove to her house, which was a little bit outside of town. When I got there, the party had started and people were already drunk, or stoned, or both. Karen welcomed me and introduced me to her best friends, Mike and Brady."

She paused.

"I'm sorry," she said. "I still remember it all so clearly. It's difficult."

It was my turn to take her hand in mine. She didn't withdraw it.

"We chatted. We drank. I felt wonderful. It got late. People began leaving the party, but Karen insisted I stay. One last drink, she said. It was spiked. Suddenly, I didn't know where I was, who I was or what was going on. I felt myself being helped up some stairs, dropped on a bed, my skirt pulled up and my panties pulled down. Karen was holding my arms while Mike and Brady were taking turns. They forced more alcohol down my throat, until I lost consciousness.

"When I woke up, I was in the back of my own car, with Karen driving and following Mike's car. I was so drunk and drugged I couldn't move or say anything. We arrived at a small cliff a few miles south of here. They dragged me out, put me behind the wheel, turned on the engine and pushed the car over the cliff.

"Miraculously, I survived. I got a broken back, third degree burns on my legs and my body and spent almost six months in a coma, but I survived."

"I'm so sorry," I said, feeling the obscene emptiness of these words at the very second I uttered them.

"There was a trial, of course. But the boys said I had been asking them for sex, and Karen said she was downstairs all the time, partying with everybody else. She had many witnesses, who also saw me climb into my car alone. To add to the obscenity, Brady told the court he had offered to drive me back because I was 'so obviously drunk and stoned'. They were all acquitted. My parents decided to leave the town."

The summer sun seemed obscenely garish now, coloring everything a joyous yellow.

"I went to university, got a degree in chemistry and specialized in botany. I made a little fortune by creating Flower Life, and a few years ago I began to think of my revenge. The first step for me was to come back, and this house was perfect for me. It was the most expensive and visible house in the town, and its color was the color of blood."

"How did Karen, Mike and Brady react when you came back?"

"I don't think they ever knew who I was. If they did, I never heard anything about it. Clara at the supermarket is my eyes and ears—she was one of the few girls who talked to me in high school, and who showed support during the trial. All they knew was that I was an 'entitled crippled black bitch' and that I was buying up property they had their eyes on. Maybe they suspected something, but who cares? It's too late now."

She had a crooked smile that made me feel uncomfortable.

"The second step was finding a way to get my revenge. Sure, buying up property and letting it rot is good. It makes the town suffer. But it takes time, it's symbolic and it doesn't really pay for what happened to me, to poor Thea-Louise and all the sorry souls who have been long forgotten. And that's where you step in, my dear."

I waited, both fascinated and appalled by the stories I was hearing.

"I have always believed in the power of dreams, just as I believe in the power of plants. The latter have made me rich, the first have brought me what I was looking for: Thea-Louise and you."

69

"I think I will have that glass of water now, if you don't mind," I said, getting up.

"There is spring water in the fridge, the glasses are in the cupboard above the sink."

I poured some of the icy liquid into a glass, and downed it in a long gulp. My throat was parched. I felt like running away, and yet I knew that Lizzie's warning was true: if I fled, I would never have an explanation, as crazy as it might be. And what was worse? Something impossible you could reject with all the strength of your reason, or something that would haunt you forever, leaving you in a cursed in-between? Choosing the first solution, I took my seat in front of Lizzie Nielsen again.

70

Lizzie patted the thick volume on the coffee table with a caring hand.

"I began to collect all the info I could on this town since I was in college. This book comes from my great-great-grandpa. He started it. It stops here."

She lifted a couple of pages.

"The rest was filled by me. Anecdotes, accidents, murders, everything that went on in this town. I was interested in finding more about Thea-Louise, but it proved impossible. If you tried to google her on the Web, you won't find anything."

I nodded.

"Her tomb was paid for by my great-great-grandpa, just so you know. I was very frustrated, because I felt close to her and her story. I wanted her to help me get my revenge, because I had a hunch she could. Don't ask me how, I just knew it. And then, I discovered your novels, with the wonderful Ada Faraday and her dream powers. I began studying dreams, downloading everything I could find on my Kindle. I studied dream magic too, and I became an expert. Dreams make people meet, dreams reveal the future, dreams can also provoke 'coincidences'. Do you see what I'm getting at?"

"No, not really," I lied, knowing perfectly well where this conversation was leading and not really wanting to hear it, although I knew I *had* to hear it.

"Thea-Louise began to appear in my dreams, and we chatted. Of course, as you know, she is mentally impaired, but I could feel her anger, I could feel her rage. It was like mine and much, much older than mine, which meant ten times as powerful. We agreed that we should make this town suffer and punish the monsters for what they had done. Unfortunately, Thea-Louise was a powerless ghost, and me a useless cripple.

"I read a lot, and I love horror, as you might have guessed. When I read your wonderful Ada Faraday stories, and the way

SEB DOUBINSKY

you described how dreams worked in such a precise and perfect fashion, I was very impressed. Then the "coincidences" happened: your car crash, and an interview you gave a few months later, stating you wanted to write in a peaceful place by the sea."

"I remembered this interview. I was completely depressed, and yes, I meant what I said. The following day, I began searching for a place to rent, possibly near the ocean."

"As you know, things worked out and fell into place. And Thea-Louise and I finally had our instrument of vengeance: you, my dear."

I rubbed my eyes with my fingers, trying to make sense of the impossible.

"You mean, you set me up in renting your cabin? But how? Telepathy? Spells? How?"

I was oscillating between being furious and exploding into hysterical laughter. Lizzie bent forward and put her hand on my forehead. The gesture had a surprisingly calming effect.

"Dear, dear, we can say that either my magic worked, or that it was an incredible coincidence. We will never know, and we can both choose what suits us best. Such is the richness of life."

I nodded stupidly, as if her hand had neutralized my anger. A question was growing in my mouth, but I didn't know how to formulate it.

"I know what you want to ask me, dear. Go ahead."

"Did I kill these people? I mean, *really?*"

Lizzi sighed.

"The gun and poison kill their victims, but are they guilty? I am guilty, and so is Thea-Louise. You are just an instrument. An object. No one can condemn you. No one. Would you sentence a gun? A bottle of poison? It wouldn't make any sense, right?"

She laughed.

"Justice has been done. A sentence has been passed. The guilty have been punished. You should feel proud, not depressed. You have helped me and Thea-Louise. You're a good man. A really good man."

"I am an accessory to murder," I growled.

"If you want, yes. But no one can prove it," Lizzie stated. "Now you can go all Dostoevsky and kill yourself because you

130

can't live with it, or continue being a decent human being who has had some terribly frightening nightmares. Sometimes we have to see the larger picture and accept our tiny role, even if it seems morally wrong. Some call it karma, other divine justice, or whatever they want. I simply call it the way of all things."

"If what you say is true, you used me. I can't accept that!"

"You can see it like that. One could also say that you were meant to be used, that everything led you here in order for you to achieve your destiny. We needed you and you needed the violence. You needed to liberate yourself from the darkness that was surrounding you, from all the injustice that had befallen you."

"I... What? How can you say that?"

"Can you really tell me you didn't enjoy what you did? Just a little bit?"

She smirked and I rubbed my face with my hands. I could remember precisely how I felt when I had crushed Karen's skull and thrown the Zippo into the wrecked car's cabin. I could remember and I didn't want to.

I stood up in the golden summer light seeping through the curtains.

"I will be leaving today, Lizzie," I said. "Thank you very much for the talk and your hospitality. The rest, I'll figure out myself."

"It was wonderful meeting you in the flesh," Lizzie said in good humor. "All the pleasure is mine. And I am looking forward to reading your next novel. I feel honored you wrote it here. It's going to be a classic, I can feel it."

She winked at me and I left her sitting in her comfortable armchair, bathed in sunshine.

Back at the cabin, I called Bill to tell him I had finished the first draft of the novel and that I was coming back tonight. I made a plane reservation, packed everything in a rush and drove the rental back to the airport. When I finally stepped into the familiar space of my apartment, I burst into tears. But they were not tears of despair this time. They were tears of relief.

EPILOGUE

The late autumn sun is setting over the city. The red brick buildings are turning orange under the darkening blue sky. A few clouds display psychedelic hues. I stare out of the window of my flat, a whisky in my hand, the pipe stuck in the corner of my mouth. Later, I will meet Bill and his husband at a new Asian restaurant. He wants to introduce me to a new writer he is representing. I have seen her picture in an online literary magazine. She writes horror too. I think he wants to hook me up with her.

The day has been busy. This morning I saw my new shrink, who says I am making progress. It is not the one my ex-wife recommended, but he is very good. My afternoon was spent signing a pile of *Hexen* copies in Bill's office. The book will launch this weekend. There are already rumors of a film deal.

My thoughts drift back to Lizzie Nielsen and Thea-Louise, but I switch them off. No need to linger on craziness. Whatever happened happened, and some doors are better never re-opened. I don't have bad dreams anymore, and I don't see a murderer every time I look at myself in a mirror like I did a few months ago, but I do often ask myself how guilty a revolver would feel if it had a soul.

I sip a drop of my whisky and keep staring at the sun, the streets, the cars, the shop windows, the passersby and I wonder if, after all, "reality" is not just a careless dream we deliberately choose to live in, knowing how ridiculously powerless we become when confronted to the horror hiding behind the facade of our skin.

Seb Doubinsky is a bilingual French dystopian writer and poet. He is the author of the "City-States Cycle", comprising, among others, *The Babylonian Trilogy*, *The Song Of Synth*, *Missing Signal*, *The Invisible* and *Paperclip*. *Missing Signal*, published by Meerkat Press, won the Bronze Foreword Reviews Award in the Best Science-Fiction Novel category in 2018. He lives in Denmark with his family and teaches literature, history and culture in the French department of Aarhus University.